SPECIAL MESSAGE TO READERS

This book is published by

THE ULVERSCROFT FOUNDATION

a registered charity in the U.K., No. 264873

The Foundation was established in 1974 to provide funds to help towards research, diagnosis and treatment of eye diseases. Below are a few examples of contributions made by THE ULVERSCROFT FOUNDATION:

A new Children's Assessment Unit at Moorfield's Hospital, London.

•

Twin operating theatres at the Western Ophthalmic Hospital, London.

•

The Frederick Thorpe Ulverscroft Chair of Ophthalmology at the University of Leicester.

•

Eye Laser equipment to various eye hospitals.

If you would like to help further the work of the Foundation by making a donation or leaving a legacy, every contribution, no matter how small, is received with gratitude. Please write for details to:

THE ULVERSCROFT FOUNDATION,
The Green, Bradgate Road, Anstey,
Leicester LE7 7FU. England

Telephone: (0533) 364325

Love is
a time of enchantment:
in it all days are fair and all fields
green. Youth is blest by it,
old age made benign: the eyes of love see
roses blooming in December,
and sunshine through rain. Verily
is the time of true-love
a time of enchantment – and
Oh! how eager is woman
to be bewitched!

DR. LEE'S RETURN

Even when she saw the letter Lisa Lee felt uneasy – and she was right. Her husband's father was ill and Andrew was needed to take over his father's practice. In the little coastal town life quickly changed from the idyllic style she was used to, for every way she turned she came up against an uneasy silence. Andrew, who had been a widower, never spoke of his first wife, and neither did anyone else. Why would nobody talk about the past?

Books by Kathleen Treves
in the Ulverscroft Large Print Series:

I'LL WAIT BELOVED
ORPHAN HOUSE
TOMORROW WEARS A VEIL
FROSTED WINDOWS
WHEN THE HEART SPEAKS
THE BRAVE OF HEART
WITHOUT YOUR LOVE
AFRAID TO LOVE
THIS WAY TO MY HEART
YOU BELONG TO ME

KATHLEEN TREVES

DR. LEE'S RETURN

Complete and Unabridged

ULVERSCROFT
Leicester

First published in Great Britain by
Ward Lock & Co. Limited
London

First Large Print Edition
published August 1991

British Library CIP Data

Treves, Kathleen, *1913–*
Dr. Lee's return.—Large print ed.—
Ulverscroft large print series: romance
I. Title
823.914 [F]

ISBN 0–7089–2489–1

Published by
F. A. Thorpe (Publishing) Ltd.
Anstey, Leicestershire

Set by Words & Graphics Ltd.
Anstey, Leicestershire
Printed and bound in Great Britain by
T. J. Press (Padstow) Ltd., Padstow, Cornwall

1

LISA brushed her soft brown hair in front of the dressing-table mirror, and watched her husband. They had been married such a little while and had been so happy. And now the letter had come, and she wasn't sure of anything any more.

It had come this morning, with his other mail. He had been laughing gently at her across the table, turning over the pile of letters, and she had been watching him then, and had seen his face change when he recognised the handwriting, and saw the Queensmarket stamp.

Instinctively she had distrusted the sight of that letter when she had picked it up off the mat. Childishly she had hidden it at the bottom of the pile, dreading the moment when he should see it. She didn't know why she had done this except that the name 'Queensmarket' had sounded like a dread knell of doom in her head.

All she knew about Queensmarket was that it hugged the coast in East Anglia, and that her beloved Andrew had his roots there. He had mentioned it once or twice, and she had seen it on his Birth Certificate, but he himself hadn't talked of it. His very reticence about the place had given it a rather sinister significance, she thought, as she brushed her hair and wished she could be sure that he had married her for the same reason that she had married him: for love.

She loved him with an intensity that was as much an aching yearning as a positive sense of happiness. She waited for his return from the hospital in the evenings with a queer foreboding that something would happen to take him from her. It left her while he was with her but, the moment he said goodbye in the morning, it was there again.

She knew it wasn't reasonable, and she was terrified that he would find out and think she was possessive. He had a safe job, doing research at his old hospital. She knew where he was every hour of the day, as surely as if he had worked in an office. Yet from the first day of their marriage, she had had this savage dread of losing him.

"Haven't you brushed your hair enough?" he said, mildly. There was a tender note in his voice, a quizzical smile touching his sensitive well-moulded mouth, but she saw it as the kindness of a man who was always kind to those younger than himself. She was inclined to be over-conscious of the discrepancy of years between them – thirteen years – in spite of his insistence that they didn't matter.

"Come and sit down and let me tell you about what I've been thinking all day long," he said, patting the seat beside him. He liked to sit on the student couch that ran along the base of their big divan bed. "Come along, dearest, because there's a lot to discuss and I have to get up early."

She came unwillingly and sat down by him, her brown eyes wary.

"It's that letter, isn't it?" she said.

"You've been worrying about it all day. Poor sweet," he said, taking her chin in his hand and pushing her long hair back. It was soft and straight, and just reached below her shoulders, and she had a short thick fringe that made her look even younger than she was. "You're such a baby," he said, kissing the tip of her nose. "I don't know how you keep those brats in order."

He was referring to her music pupils. Music was the one thing they didn't share.

"They're all right," she said, impatiently, wanting to know now about the letter because it was assuming menacing proportions. "The letter, Andrew."

"Oh, yes. That letter. It was from my father," he said, drawing himself up, letting her chin go, and stretching out his long legs in front of him. "As you know, he's a G.P. in Queensmarket."

He stood up. He was so tall, and the bedside lamp threw his shadow right across the room and up the wall. Tall and dark and lean and distinguished. A clever-looking man, a strong man.

"I haven't told you much about him, have I? Or about my background. I suppose I should have done. But it was so nice as things are – us here, living so conveniently near the hospital and my work, and you with your music. It seemed a shame to disturb it all."

He sighed and came back to stand in front of her.

"He isn't young any more, my father. He fell down a steep, dark staircase in a patient's house some time ago, and now he can't carry on the practice." He drew a deep breath and forced himself to continue. "He wants me to go home and take his place."

Lisa couldn't take it in at first. "Wants you to go home, Andrew? But when?"

"At once, of course. I can get released from the hospital and it'll be a chance for you and my father to get to know each other. It isn't as if we were going to the ends of the earth, Lisa," he urged. "We're just going back to my home town."

"But why do we have to go back, Andrew?" Lisa asked, with a catch in her voice. "I mean, what's wrong with a *locum tenens*? Or selling the practice to someone else?"

Dr. Lee looked at his young wife rather helplessly. He was still holding the letter from his father. He sat down again, the letter between them, and tried to explain.

"Darling, try to understand. This is

a suburb of London. People live here, and go about their business, and move, and no-one is unduly put out. It's all impersonal, d'you see? But my father's practice is in Queensmarket, and people care — really care — that old Dr. Lee can't attend them any more since his accident. Lees have been in the Old House for two hundred years. It would be unthinkable for me not to go back and carry on the practice."

"Suppose you hadn't been a doctor," she objected.

"Well, then, that would have been different, because I couldn't have gone back to help him if I hadn't been a doctor, now could I?" He said it with a smile but with the patient voice of an adult reasoning with a child. "But, as I am a doctor, then I must. I owe it to my father, too. He's been so good to me — in every phase of my life," he finished, with quiet conviction.

She glanced quickly at him. Was he referring to the time of his first marriage, she wondered?

He had never talked of his first wife. It was tacitly agreed between them that

that first marriage of his should remain a closed book. He had always said that he wouldn't go back to places he had known before, too, but she refused to remind him of that now. What concerned her more was why he should feel he *could* go back to Queensmarket, after his former reluctance.

He smiled uncertainly at her, and she noticed how tired and lined his face was today. He was thirty-five, but at this moment he looked older than his years. Worry about his father, she supposed. That lick of grey in his dark brown hair was so marked at this moment, but it was still a distinguished face. She had hoped so much that he would stay at his hospital in London and continue his research work, because that was where his heart was, she felt instinctively. And now, all of a sudden, he was deciding to go into general practice.

"Queensmarket is a very nice town really, Lisa," he said, with cheerfulness he didn't feel. "Let me show you these pictures. I got them out of the bureau. I'm sure if you were to see what it looked like you would feel better about it."

"But how long would we be there?" she asked faintly. "What about my music pupils? What about this house?"

He looked surprised, put out. He had, for the moment, overlooked that aspect.

It was Lisa's house. A small, semi-detached one, left to her by her parents. The house they had moved into while she had been still at school. She had an affection for it. It was cosy, in a street of similarly cosy houses, where some of her young pupils lived. Here were her roots. It had been while she was visiting one of her young pupils in hospital that she had met Andrew. And it was on the doorstep of the West End, with its theatres and taxis and familiar big shops and various other entertaining interests. Concerts and exhibitions and music shops and books – what could this small town of Queensmarket offer to compare with these things that meant so much to her?

Andrew looked bothered. He abstractedly reached across and took her hand.

"I rather hoped – well, my dearest, I must continue the practice but, if you want to keep this house on, to come here for week-ends, or to stay here by yourself – "

He left it in the air, anguish on his face. It struck her that when he had decided that he must of course throw up everything and go to help his father, he had fully expected Lisa to come too. When they had married, he had fallen in with her suggestion to live in her house. She taught music from there and, anyway, it was more comfortable for him than to stay on in Residence, and certainly far less trouble than to go flat-hunting.

"Had you forgotten my music pupils?" she asked in a small voice. "I can't just leave them, can I?"

Her music. The one thing they didn't share.

"We don't need the money, my dear, but if you feel you must go on teaching music, why not in Queensmarket? I believe there are small children there," he added, in a touching attempt at a joke.

She tried to echo his smile but her brown eyes mirrored her troubled state. Everything in her was resisting this removal to Queensmarket. Purely instinctive, the feeling grew and grew with every second.

Ever since the letter had come that morning, and Andrew had read it to himself over breakfast, it had been growing into a mountain of foreboding. All he had said was that it was from his father who had been ill and he added that he would tell her about it when he came home . . . there wasn't time at that moment. He had gone to the hospital, anxiety in his eyes, and on his return tonight he said at last, "Could you bear it if I said we were going to leave London?"

It was impossible for her to make up her mind about whether Andrew wanted to go or whether he was being driven to it from sheer duty. And they had been married too short a time for her to ask him the blunt question. She was so conscious of her position as second wife.

She found herself being careful of everything she said and did, for fear it fell short of the standard set by his first wife, the one who had died. She had heard other people say that it was usually like this. She had read about it in books.

She faced the question squarely and honestly, and was convinced that if it had been she who now had a husband following Andrew, she would always have been comparing them both. Andrew was the first man she had ever loved, but what if there had been the second man in her life? How much could she have loved someone, after Andrew? How much did he love her?

"It's not a large town," Andrew went on, seeming to warm to the subject as he turned over the snapshots, the coloured postcards, and a guide-book. "Mostly Queen Anne houses, and very old shop fronts, some with bottle glass in the bow windows. Look at this one: Martin Biddell's – he's the chemist. Nice chap. Oh, look, here's one of my home. This is The Old House. Now, how do you feel about living there, Lisa?"

It had a flat white front, and a deep porch with stone pillars. A neat flagged path went in a straight line to the pavement. Dignified railings kept in the small shrub-filled garden. An old-fashioned metal arch over the gate, with a big lamp in it – presumably a red one – indicated that it was a doctor's house. Connected to The Old House was the wall of the chemist's shop and, looming above them both, was a lighthouse.

"Oh, it isn't right behind them," Andrew said quickly, laughing a little. "It's on the shore, but it looks as close as that."

"I didn't know Queensmarket would be like that, with a *lighthouse*!" Lisa said blankly. "I suppose I didn't expect a holiday resort with summer visitors and all that."

"Oh, but it isn't. It's near the coast, but it's not seaside – no hotels or funfairs, or bathing huts or anything like that, just the shore, sand-dunes, sea-wall, the lighthouse – look, here's a picture we – I mean, I took, some years ago."

He looked bothered at that slip he had made, and didn't meet her eyes. Who was the other half of the 'we?' His first wife?

He didn't make any attempt at explanation and she didn't feel that she could ask him.

"This is the park," he went on, without a pause. "Not a public park. More of a memorial garden to the town's fallen in the two wars. It was privately donated by the Mawson family. They all went away except Carmichael. I was at school with him."

He sounded now as if he were on safer ground.

"What does he do now?" she asked, feeling she ought to say something, so that the sound of her own voice should reassure her, because it now occurred to her that all these people, these houses, this town, must have been familiar with that shadowy figure who had been in Lisa's shoes before her. Andrew's first wife. Lisa didn't even know her name.

She didn't know much about her at all, really. Only that she had existed, belonged to him, filled his thoughts so that even now there were blank moments when he seemed to retreat to some other place where Lisa couldn't reach him, and where she could only feel that he was with that other woman still.

"This man, this Carmichael Mawson," she said gently, putting her hand on his, "what does he do now?"

"Oh, he farms," Andrew Lee said, with an effort, pulling his thoughts back from heaven knew where.

As if he realised suddenly that he had left her, he put out his hand to touch her soft cheek.

"Lisa, I don't know what you must think of me for wanting to uproot you like this. It's caught me unprepared."

"But," she pointed out, "you didn't say we were to leave London when that letter came this morning. I thought it was just bad news. I thought you might even want to go and see your father but I didn't expect you to say we'd got to go at once and live there!"

"No, but since then I've been on the telephone to – well, to an old friend, to find out just what the position is, and she shocked me with her news about my father. I always thought of him as such a strong man but it seems that, since his accident, his health has broken. He isn't the same. I wasn't going to tell you this. No new bride wants to have to look after an invalid. I thought perhaps we ought to go and see, stay for a little while and see how things worked out. But, of course, that won't do. You must go, prepared to stay. That's what he wants. You do see, sweet, don't you?"

2

LISA felt lost and bewildered. In the next few days so many changes took place. First there was the question of the house.

"I do want to keep it," she said faintly. "Just as it is. I mean, we might want to come to London for a week-end. I suppose we could, couldn't we?"

"Is that the only reason you want to keep it, Lisa?" he asked her, very gently turning her face to his and searching it, as if he expected to be able to find the truth there.

She felt, as she did on occasions such as this, that he could read her thoughts; that there was nothing really private. His eyes could be so penetrating and, in a queer way, she resented it, much as she loved him, because to him she was an open book, but to her he had revealed so little, and his face gave so little away.

Because of this tiny flame of resentment she was at once ashamed, over-eager to make up for it even after it was banished, so she said, "No. No, not really, except that it's mine but, if you want to put it on the market, you can sell it. I don't mind."

In the end, after a lot of discussion about it, he suggested that the house should be left as it was, for the time being.

"But someone ought to keep looking in, cleaning it up, Lisa."

"Mrs. Cobb might be glad to," Lisa said, overwhelmed with relief. She had wanted to feel that there was someone else she could go to, someone not alien, if the atmosphere of Queensmarket became too much for her. The feeling worried her but she didn't stop to analyse it then, beyond thinking that almost every new wife probably felt the same when faced with the prospect of an in-law she didn't really know and the husband's home town which she hadn't even seen.

"I thought Mrs. Cobb was going to Australia to her son?" Andrew came back to say.

"She was. She'd sold up, and was waiting, but there's been a hitch. Now she's staying at No. 9 with Mrs. Green. They've always been friends."

"But the Green house was already bursting at the seams. Where on earth did they put the old lady to sleep?"

"She's not all that old," Lisa protested, "and, anyway she's on the studio couch in the sitting-room but she doesn't like it much because it's so noisy, what with 'pop' records and the twins – they're very noisy boys really."

"Perhaps she'd like to come and sleep here,"Andrew suggested. "She could have her board and lodging in return for keeping the house in order."

Mrs. Cobb was delighted with the arrangement and set about moving in the next day. She hadn't much to move, just two battered cases. Her trunk was roped and ready.

She was a wiry spare little woman with a tremendous fund of hope and cheerfulness. She looked searchingly at Lisa as she took her hat off, and remarked, "Well, you could have knocked me down with a feather when you first suggested this idea to me, my dear. Not only because it's such a godsend to me but because, well, when I heard that the doctor had to go back and take on his father's practice, I made sure there'd be a sale board going up outside this house. We all did."

"I couldn't bear to let it go. Not yet, anyway. My parents lived here, you see," Lisa said.

"Ah, yes, that do make a mort of difference. I know just how you feel, duck. Never been the same since they went, so Mrs. Green tells me. Of course, me living at the other end of the bus route, as you might say, I didn't know 'em so well, but I can understand your feelings. Still, you've got a nice father-in-law, haven't you? What's he like? Like the doctor?"

Lisa was ashamed to say she didn't know. "We haven't seen him, not since the wedding. I did meet him that once, and he was rather like my husband, I suppose."

"Oh. Oh, well, I'm sure he's nice."

Mrs. Cobb made a cup of tea. It was good tea, strong and sweet, and they sat drinking it in the kitchen.

"What about the wife?" Mrs. Cobb asked suddenly.

To Lisa, who had been thinking about

the first Mrs. Andrew Lee, and had been far away in her thoughts, the last person she expected Mrs. Cobb to be talking about was Andrew's mother. So she said rather defensively and looking faintly shocked, "Well, I didn't know her, did I?"

"Oh, she's dead, is she, my dear? Well, between you and me, it's as well, to my way of thinking. You've both lost your mothers, and that makes it even, and in almost all cases a man's mother is a nuisance to his young bride. I well remember my mother-in-law — "

Again Lisa was swamped with relief. Why had she thought Mrs. Cobb would be talking about the first wife? It was very unlikely that she would even know that Andrew had been married before. Lisa hadn't told the neighbours much about him. But, of course, they would all know — they would have seen the announcement in the newspapers about them at the time of the wedding. Why it had been necessary to mention that Andrew was a widower, she couldn't think. Probably to make it more interesting. A young widower. The poor first wife . . .

"Yes, well, I've got an awful lot to do," Lisa said hastily scrambling to her feet. "Thank you for the tea. I'm going to the hairdressers now. We shall be leaving here tonight as soon as my husband comes homes so, if I don't get another chance to speak to you, I hope you'll soon have good news about your passage to Australia, and thank you very much indeed for helping us out like this."

"Supposing I hear pretty soon?" Mrs. Cobb said. "I expect you'll want me to recommend someone else to take my place, won't you? I know someone — someone honest, who'd love the chance."

"All right, and thank you,." Lisa said desperately. Now she wondered whether she had done the right thing. She had kept one foot in this quiet street where everyone knew her and, even though it was a bolt-hole to come back to, if she did come back they would all want to know why; all know her business . . .

"Well, it's either to do this or cut it off clean," she told herself sharply, but the idea of cutting it off clean, selling up the home she had made at No. 19, and resigning herself to the unknown future in Queensmarket, appalled her.

She gave herself no chance to think, during that day. There was not only her hair to have set, but there were warm casual clothes to buy – the sort of clothes she never had the need to wear in London. And there was the question of her pupils. Most of them she had placed with two nearby teachers, but there was still Bertie Joiner's mother to see and to persuade her to let him go on with his lessons. A change of teacher was a good opportunity for Bertie's mother to stop his music, and turn the money to what she called 'better account,' which really meant taking up some new hire purchase account. Bertie's mother was known to have her eye on a new three-piece suite for the best room.

Lisa sighed. She hated giving up her own pupils and she couldn't believe that she, a newcomer, could find new ones in Queensmarket. How could you teach music in a doctor's house?

She was tired when she reached home. Andrew got there at the same time, in his newest car – a rather nice grey one, not opulent, but adequate. He got out with a smile.

"You're home late, my dear. You look exhausted. Where have you been? I expected you to be ready to start."

He had forgotten about Bertie Joiner's mother, of course. Her music and the pupils just didn't impress him as being more than a pleasant hobby with her.

So she contented herself with saying, "I got held up. We can start right away, can't we?"

"Have you eaten?"

She brushed aside his solicitous question with a nod. No sense in admitting that she had had nothing since lunch-time, because if he found out then that she had been to see the mother of one of his pupils, he would be angry. He already felt that she gave too much time to the children.

"Then that's all right," he said, and they went in together.

Mrs. Cobb met them in the hall. The luggage was stacked ready. Mrs. Cobb helped them carry it out, and watched Andrew pack it in the boot and the smaller cases on the back seat. She chuckled.

"I daresay by the time I come back from Australia to visit all my old friends (as I shall do after three years) I'll find you'll be stacking that back seat with other things."

"Other things?" Lisa echoed blankly, pausing to look in sharp surprise at Andrew's sudden drawn countenance.

"That's right," Mrs. Cobb said heartily. "Things like a carry-cot and a car seat and a hold-all. Must have a handy bag with waterproof lining. Oh, you don't know my dear, what a lot of fun you've got coming. And I wish you the very best, straight I do. Both of you, if I may say so, doctor. And many thanks for putting me up like this until — "

"Thank *you*," Andrew said tautly, cutting her off in mid-stream, "but we really must be off."

Lisa waited until the car was roaring up the quiet street and the last neighbour had stopped waving, before she asked him why he had cut Mrs. Cobb off like that.

"Let's say I don't care for all the flag-waving, just because we're going to my home," he said.

"Andrew!" she protested. "But they're

the neighbours. My friends. Isn't it like that in your home town?"

"No." The negative was as taut as a whiplash. She recoiled, her hand tensed and gripping her handbag on her lap until the knuckles showed white. He saw them out of the corner of his eye.

"I'm sorry, sweet, but it's been a trying day, passing over all my notes and initiating the chap who's taking my place, and other things I had to do as well. And I'm not enjoying the thought of going to live in Queensmarket any more than you are."

"Then why do we have to go?" she asked. "I mean, couldn't you have really put someone else in?"

"We've gone all over that before, Lisa. Done the subject to death. I suppose I shouldn't have admitted that I didn't want to go back. I've tried to keep all that a closed book – honestly I have. It wasn't fair to you to have it all dragged out again. But what could I do? *What could I do*?"

The last sentence was uttered in a low tone but she felt that it was being forced out of him.

"Andrew, don't you think you ought to tell me about it?"

Now he was on the defensive again. "There's nothing to tell, Lisa. Just because I'm one of those people who just don't like going back, I don't really have to make all this fuss. I suppose, if the truth were known, I feel helpless before Fate, making a situation where I have to do something I don't want to. I've never liked that. I prefer to choose my own way and stick to it."

"But why did you look so awful just now at poor Mrs. Cobb? She was only thinking that we'd probably have started a family in three years' time. Well, we might, mightn't we?"

He didn't answer to that. Lisa didn't notice then, being swept on by other things he was saying, but later she was to remember and to wonder.

"She's an old busybody," he snorted. "And whatever she may have been thinking, she should have kept her thoughts to herself."

The silence deepened between them after that, and they had gone through the northern outskirts of London and were on the road to Colchester before he spoke again.

"Forgive me, Lisa. I had no right to snap at you like that. I was just worried. Wondering what sort of state my father is in and, what is more to the point, what sort of state the practice is in. And, of course, how you fit in."

"Never mind," she comforted him. "We shall both be new to it, shan't we?"

Again there was a silence and then he said, "But didn't I tell you? I've been in general practice before. I used to be my father's partner."

3

"NO, you didn't tell me," Lisa gasped. "When was this, Andrew?"

"As soon as I'd qualified," he said shortly. "It isn't important. Two other chaps in my year went into practice with their fathers. One of them stuck it; the other one finished up as a ship's doctor. It depends on the chap himself and, of course on his father. Mine, as you'll soon see, likes to be master of his own household."

"But will you be able to get on with him now, Andrew, if you couldn't get on with him then? And is that why he didn't show much interest in me – because you had a row with him?"

"No, you don't understand. I didn't quarrel with him. I just – well, I just couldn't stand it any longer. I wanted to get away. I spent a year doing locum jobs all over the country – it wasn't much of a life, I may add, but it gave me breathing-space. And then I went into research."

So, she reasoned, he was with his father on qualifying. Where did that first marriage fit in? Now it was imperative to ask him. She must know.

But Andrew, in effect, told her, although he may not have realised it. "The years in research were lonely but rewarding ones. I liked research. I liked living alone in residence – until I met you, of course. It's been fun, Lisa, hasn't it?"

"It has for me," she said, with a catch in her voice. "Ever since I first met you, Andrew, six months ago, life has changed. I used to wish it could never end. It's been so nice. But how about you? How nice was it really?"

"Don't dissect it, darling. Just take it from me, it's been very nice."

"I wasn't going to dissect it, Andrew, but a woman likes to know, sometimes, how much she's – that is, how her husband feels about her."

"I've said it's been nice, so that means I've found you all that I desired you to be," he said, with patience. Patience in Andrew was a thing to be avoided. He was kind, usually, and carelessly affectionate; preoccupied, peaceful, upset and furious – all the extremes but, of all his moods, she had found his mood of patience the one to be avoided. If she didn't avoid it, he tended to drift away into that world in which she had no entry, and she felt she had lost him. The world from which he came back, with blank eyes, and stared at her, as if trying to remember who she was and why she was there.

"Sorry, Andrew. Didn't mean to press you for information, but," she said, in a rush, swallowing her pride, "I do love you so much, and it would be heavenly to hear you say you loved me – just once."

After a startled silence he laughed, softly, indulgently.

"What a lot of extravagant words, my darling. And it's all nonsense. Of course you wouldn't be content hearing it just once. I'd have to say it every week and then it would get down to every day, and too much of a good thing is fatal."

So, as always, he had dismissed it as a joke, and she still didn't know why he had married her, or whether in fact he loved her at all.

It was dark when they reached Queensmarket. Lisa was very disappointed. She had wanted to see the town in daylight and not to wake up in the centre of it.

It was very cold, and the moment she got out of the car the salt tang of sea water struck her nostrils. The lighthouse beam flickered rhythmically from above their heads, and below, all the lights in the The Old House were on.

Andrew looked worried. "Come on, let's hurry. I wonder what's happened?"

A dumpy little woman with rosy apple cheeks opened the door to his knock.

"Well, Master Andy, then how are you, how are you?" she said, in a thick, husky, jolly voice. Her little blue eyes twinkled and she clutched at Andrew with her fat arms, as if for two pins she would hug him. Then she remembered her place, and stepped back, smoothing down her dress and banishing the wide smile. "I forgot. It's the Madam with you, isn't it?"

"Yes, Mrs. Tabb, this is Lisa, my . . . wife."

It was queer and chilling, the way he hesitated over the word. Lisa glanced at him and then at the housekeeper.

"Good evening, Mrs. Tabb," she said.

Her young face was tremulous, white with fatigue, and there was an emotion in it that Mrs. Tabb wrote off in her mind as fear. What, she asked herself, had this girl-bride to be afraid of?

"Why, she's nought but a babe," she said, laughing a little, and giving Lisa a brief hug. "There, how can I treat you with respect when you're nothing but a child, wanting a good hot supper and bed? There now, nought but a babe," she said again and, cocking her bright eye at Andrew, she started to say, "Not like . . . " and then broke off uncertainly, again her smile fading.

Lisa looked round at Andrew and found the tail-end of a frown and shake of the head. Why had he stopped Mrs. Tabb from speaking? Who had she been going to refer to?

"Why are all the lights on, Mrs. Tabb?" Andrew asked, with a swift change of the conversation.

"Just a bit of a welcome, my love," she told him.

"Oh," he sounded relieved. "I thought perhaps my father might be worse."

They went in, Mrs. Tabb talking all the while about the old doctor.

"It's most vexing, that accident of his, Master Andy, and I could give that Palmer woman a piece of my mind for not seeing to a new lamp bulb, for that was all it was! For the want of a new lamp bulb the doctor goes and falls down those stairs, and look how he's been ever since! Oh, it fair makes my blood boil, for you know very well, Master Andy, he was spry for his age. Always fit and hearty, and if there was a cold to be took in a north-easter, it was me, not him!"

"Is he so very frail then, Mrs. Tabb?" Andrew asked in a low voice. They stood in the hall speaking about the doctor before they went into the room where presumably he waited for them, and Lisa was for the moment forgotten.

"Well, it's queer. Sometimes I've a mind to think all the life has been knocked out of him and sometimes, the saints forgive me, I'm catching myself thinking that he's just playing us all up, for I'd be the first to admit that, when he's in one of his tempers, his voice is as strong as ever it was. Anyway, come along in and see him. Oh, and look at us talking, and forgetting this poor child. Come along then, Miss Lisa, do. – You don't mind if I call you that? – I always call this bad lad Master Andy, seeing as I've near brought him up, and I'm not going to find it easy to call you Mrs. Lee, that I'm not."

And again she paused, as if she had said something wrong, and looked uncertainly at Andrew, before she went on.

"Doctor, it's Master Andy and the young lady," she announced, and stood back for them to go in.

It was a huge room, lined with books. Great comfortable leather and plush armchairs were dotted about and small but solid tables at the side of each. This room, Lisa was later to find, was the general sitting-room. There was a small parlour at the back, full of brocade and water colours, and a grand piano, but it was seldom used. This was the favourite room.

"Well, Andrew!" old Dr. Lee barked.

"Well, father," Andrew replied, and the two men shook hands, and Andrew sat down.

"How are you father?" he asked, automatically taking his father's wrist. The older man slapped him off.

"Don't do that!" he roared. "If I want my pulse taken I can take it myself." He looked past Andrew at Lisa and snorted. "Good heavens, she looks younger than she did at her wedding. How old are you, girl?"

"I'm twenty-two," Lisa said, quietly, and, for the life of her she couldn't add any name. She couldn't bring herself to call him 'father' and somehow Dr. Lee sounded far too formal.

She tried to examine her feelings, and all she could think of was that he was so much like a shrunken edition of Andrew that he repelled her on that score alone. It was like looking forward into the future and seeing her beloved Andrew old and tired and ill and hating it. She couldn't bear it. And she knew instinctively that for some reason old Dr. Lee didn't like her. Or if he didn't go so far as to dislike her, at least he had no room in his heart for his son's new wife.

"Well, Andrew, have you made up your mind to stay here?" Dr. Lee demanded.

"Yes, father, as I told you over the telephone today, we've talked it over, Lisa and I, and we've decided to stay and make this our home."

Dr. Lee grunted. He stared at Lisa and then he looked hard at his son.

"Does she know about . . . " he began, and broke off. Again, out of the side of her eye, Lisa caught that frown and shake of the head from Andrew.

"Oh, well, you know what you're doing, I suppose," Dr Lee growled. "And if you're going to take surgery tomorrow there's a lot to discuss."

The two men sat talking until Mrs. Tabb came in with a tray of hot coffee and scones, and carried Lisa off to see her room. The men hardly noticed her go out. They were discussing the practice, Dr. Lee's health, and how Andrew was to proceed, starting the next morning.

Mrs. Tabb bustled about cheerfully, "Well, now, my dear, and how do you think you'll like Queensmarket, eh?" she began, twinkling at Lisa.

"I'm not sure," Lisa said slowly. "Will I like it?"

Mrs. Tabb looked hard at her. "If

you're a sensible girl, and start as you mean to go on, and keep looking forward and never back, aye, I daresay you'll like it."

"What does that mean?" Lisa gasped.

"I know Master Andrew like the back of my hand," Mrs. Tabb said. "This'll be your room, and he'll be sleeping in there," and she indicated what appeared to be a small dressing-room.

Lisa stared in dismay. "Oh, but . . . " she began but Mrs. Tabb, avoiding her eyes, said firmly, "That's the way he likes it. So as not to disturb anyone else for calls in the night – and, between you and me, there are plenty. That's a thing that's been getting Dr. Lee down. There have been locums, of course, but who wants strangers? Not anyone in this town. No, it's a Lee or nobody. The old doctor's been going out, in his state of health, and one night last week, I knew he'd gone too far and I told the patient she'd better make do with her aches and pains till morning because, if she didn't, there wouldn't be a Dr. Lee to come anymore.

She folded her fat hands over her stomach. She had purposely run on, so that Lisa shouldn't break in to ask more about the habit of sleeping in that room. And then, when a break did occur, there was nothing Lisa felt she could say. It was only too clear that Mrs. Tabb had meant that in the days of the first marriage, this had been the arrangement, and it was going to be the same now.

"Was this – *her* bed?" Lisa did manage to gasp, at last. "Because if it was I don't want it."

"Her bed, my dear, was taken out and put up in the attic. It was a very ornate one, carved and padded with satin. Brought it from Italy with her after a holiday there. No, this was a new bed, bought specially to fill the gap."

To fill the gap? Lisa gasped. She need not have asked that question, then, but it had made a milestone in her life. There had been a great yawning gap to fill when Andrew's first wife had died, and they had done their best to close it in, and it was a fair guess that he had left this town because he couldn't bear to keep remembering her.

"Was she beautiful?" Lisa drove herself to ask.

"Now as to that," Mrs. Tabb said, with a fine air of indifference, "who's to say? One man's meat is another man's poison. Where one sees beauty, another might not."

"Well, did you think she was beautiful?" Lisa pressed, hardly knowing what drove her.

"I'm only the housekeeper and I keep my thoughts to myself on such a thing as that," Mrs. Tabb said firmly. "And why should you worry? Just ask yourself why he married you, and whatever the answer is, that's your strong point. Had three husbands, I have. John, the doctor's old chauffeur, Matthew, the gardener at the manor, and Gideon who was a lifeboatman. All different in their ways, they were, and what one see in me another didn't. I could tell you a thing or two about men, after the three of 'em, but I doubt if it would help you any, Miss Lisa, because you're married to Master Andrew. You've got to work out your own life."

Lisa nodded. "And it'll be all right so long as I'm not . . . in competition with a ghost," she finished on a whispered note.

Mrs. Tabb was banging the window to at the time and, whether she heard or not, she pretended she hadn't.

"What did you leave behind you in London, my dear?" she asked kindly, as she crossed the room to go to the door.

"Leave behind? Oh, friends – lots of friends, and the house I lived in before I was married. My roots," she finished, with a travesty of a smile.

"Well, there's friends and friends. It takes all sorts. As good a friend can be made here as anywhere else. And as to leaving your roots behind, that's for a tale! Some of the best growing, happy-looking plants I've ever seen have been transplanted, my dear."

4

IT was raining the next day. Andrew, who had come up to bed very late from talking with his father, had found Lisa asleep, fully dressed, sprawled across her bed. He had gently covered her with a blanket and eiderdown, and left her.

That was how she found herself the next morning. She got up stiffly and realised, to her horror, that she must have fallen asleep after lying there softly crying. Crying for her nice new marriage that had seemed so secure in her own home on the outskirts of London, but which seemed no longer secure because of that little separate room. And she herself had given impetus to the idea by falling asleep like that, right across the bed. Of course dear kind Andrew wouldn't have awakened her!

She went to the door of his room but, for some reason she couldn't define, she couldn't bring herself to open the door.

It had such a private look about it.

This was nonsense, she told herself, and sharply knocked on it, but there was no answer and, when she at last plucked up the courage to look in, it was to find it empty. Empty, with the bed stripped, Andrew's dressing-gown flung over a chair, and his clothes all over the place in their usual state of untidiness. So far as she could see, none of his clothes were missing, until she couldn't find the thick sweater and cavalry twill slacks he wore for gardening. So he had already gone out, without waking her.

It was a fine steady rain, the sort that has set in for the day, but it didn't deter Lisa.

She found the bathroom, and had a quick shower, dressed in her stretch pants, thick sweater and walking shoes, took her raincoat with her and crept downstairs.

Mrs. Tabb was already about, however, and came to the kitchen door with a good hot cup of tea.

"Here you are, my dear, get this inside of you. I knew you were about. I heard the bath water run. You'll always find a good supply of hot bath water in this house, as long as I'm here. I said to Master Andy . . ."

"Where is he?" Lisa broke in sharply.

"Now where would he be at this time of the day but out for his early morning constitutional?" Mrs. Tabb asked, in surprise.

Lisa bit back the retort that it was the first time she had heard of Andrew doing any such thing. Since their marriage he had shown a marked liking for his bed and it had been a job to get him up in the morning.

"Oh, I see," Lisa murmured, and took the cup of tea.

"You'll have a bite to eat before you go out, won't you?" Mrs. Tabb said. "I've got a nice bacon sandwich ready for you. I asked Mr. Andy if he was going to wait for you but he said he wouldn't, not this morning. If you want a nice little walk that won't get you wet through, you'd best go round the Square and have a look at the shops, get your bearings and, if you still want to go further and don't mind the rain, why then, you just go through St. Anne's Passage and take a look at the church. It's very old and quite a favourite with the summer visitors – not that we get many, mark you, but some manage to find us, way over from Skegwell, and they come and gawp at everything and buy a roll of film in Martin Biddell's and then sign the visitors book in the church and go away. Ah, there's none so queer as folk."

Lisa knew that before long she would have formed the habit of letting Mrs. Tabb run on, while her own thoughts wandered elsewhere. If you listened to everything Mrs. Tabb had to say, you'd never get a chance to think your own thoughts.

"Where is Andrew's father?" Lisa asked, with rare delicacy, avoiding calling him anything.

Mrs. Tabb looked thoughtfully at her. "In his bedroom, of course. And that's where he's going to stay until a respectable morning hour from now on, if I've got anything to do with it. Have you made up your mind what you're going to call him, then, seeing as you've no father of your own?"

"You're going to tell me what not to

call him, aren't you?" Lisa said, her face lighting up in that rare elfin grin of hers that touched her with real beauty for a fleeting moment.

Mrs. Tabb smiled in return. It wasn't possible to resist that smile of Lisa's.

"That I am," she replied heartily. "It wouldn't be wise for instance, to call him what the other one called him, now would it?"

That wiped the smile from Lisa's face. She finished her tea and put the cup down neatly on the table and waited. But, instead of telling Lisa what Dr. Lee had been called by his first daughter-in-law, she said instead; "He was only saying the other day, that he'd never been called 'Dad' in his life. Master Andy always called him 'sir' as a child, and now it's 'father'. Rather cold, to my way of thinking, but there, the good doctor doesn't exactly call up affection from people by that manner of his."

Lisa said nothing, but she felt the chill creeping back; the chill that had made her cry herself to sleep last night.

"Mind you, he's a good man," Mrs. Tabb averred. "And I think it's a pity that his own sons never realised it."

Lisa'a heart lurched.

"Sons?" she whispered. "I didn't know that Andrew had any brothers. Are they dead, then? He's never mentioned them."

Mrs. Tabb looked bothered.

"Well, they were by another marriage. I'm surprised Master Andy never mentioned them, but oh well, come to think of it, I suppose he wouldn't considering all things. Older than him, they were."

"What were their names?" Lisa asked hoarsely.

"Now don't you go taking on, Miss Lisa, and you'd better not let Master Andy know I told you. I'm sure he'd rather tell you himself. Well, I suppose you'll hear about them sooner or later, so there's not much harm in you knowing about their names, I suppose. They were twins. Quentin and Tobias."

She said it so unwillingly that Lisa felt sure they must be dead. She felt, too, that she was a stranger of strangers, probing too deeply into old wounds, for pardon. She muttered something and went out, leaving Mrs. Tabb staring into space, probably remembering those boys, and perhaps their mother.

So Dr. Lee, like his Andrew, had had two wives. What a house this was! Mrs. Tabb with her three husbands, the doctor's two wives and that first wife of Andrew's. The whole place seemed to be vibrating with their memory, and Lisa had the curious sensation of being hounded by old ghosts.

She lifted her face to the rain and took herself to task.

"What a lot of rot to talk, just because you've come to a place you don't know; that has a lot of old property and looks rather quaint," she reasoned with herself and, instead of walking round the square and looking at the shops, she turned down the first alley-way she came to.

It wasn't St.Anne's Passage. It was called Mulberry Walk, and it ambled for a long way between the backs of big houses, until it petered out behind fishermen's cottages, and a boatyard. The boatyard seemed to be exclusively for mending small craft. There wasn't a single smart piece of sea-going craft on the stocks anywhere. It was all old, and very firmly established, Lisa felt. It had all been there years and years before she had been born.

She wandered through it. There wasn't a soul about. Beyond the boatyard was a long, long cement way; hardly a promenade. Perhaps it had been once, but successive winters with their gales and high seas and battering showers of shingle had beaten the surface off it, and it was pitted and rough to the soles. Beyond the cement walk was the shore, a pitiless stretch of shingle, petering out in a rough tangle of old property. So far as she could see from here, Lisa made out boathouses, huts, beached craft sadly in need of paint, a tangle of lobster pots and a rusty winch.

Over the sea hung a white mist, almost obscuring what was left of the receding tide. Over the land the fingers of mist probed raggedly, revealing in places patches of rough grass, bare, depressing, common land, and starved trees behind.

She shivered and turned back.

Where was the park that Andrew had spoken of? Where were the sand-dunes, the quiet place for sun-bathing? Where was the sun? Would any warmth touch this unfriendly fringe of the North Sea?

Her face felt icy cold, clammy from the rain and the sea mist. She walked briskly back to the boatyard and through the passage, hoping to meet Andrew and yet somehow dreading it.

The Square looked friendly by comparison. The shops were still closed, but the air was less cold here. She did as Mrs. Tabb had suggested and walked slowly round.

Martin Biddell's shop was just like any other small chemist, except that all his goods were stuffed into the very restricted space of a bow window with bottle glass. A fierce mixture of make-up, medicines, and films jostled with proprietary brands of cures for holiday ailments, slimming aids, corn plasters and sun glasses.

Beyond the chemist was a double cottage structure, sideways to the square, approached by a neat little path. Beyond this were butcher, greengrocer, pastrycook and hardware shop. All were privately owned. A draper and hairdresser and a barber's establishment, led round the square to the far corner, where an antique shop huddled.

It was on the corner of the St.Anne's Passage that the housekeeper had said led through to the church. Beyond this again was a newsagent and post office, a dry cleaner's, an estate agent's and a stationer's where art materials were also displayed. A coy looking dress shop and milliner's and a confectioner's, a really big grocer's and a toy shop, wended their way round to the last side of the square, where private houses had been turned into offices. Solicitor, architect, two tiny branches of well-known banks, and a photographer's, jostled with a seed merchant's and pet store, a shop which sold knitting wool and an off licence.

Lisa wandered round, thinking with longing of the London shops and missing the charm of this small collection.

If you were given short change or fell out with anyone in these shops, where else would you go? They were on your door-step. They could see you come out and go in; moreover, everyone would know, she felt sure, that she was from the doctor's house.

Because the eyes of the windows of the houses in the square seemed to be staring at her, she went down yet another passage, but this was only a short one, leading into the High Street.

Here things were rather different. There semed to be more popular shops here; nothing exclusive about this lot. Branches of big stores – small branches, it was true – blared their advertisements in the windows; there was a fish-shop, and two inns called respectively the Cat and Fiddle and The Jet, and, outside the latter, was a jet plane on the signboard signifying that there was at least one establishment that realised it was the twentieth century and not the century the rest of Queensmarket seemed to slumber in.

There was a small cinema here, too, and a police station. An undertakers, which joined The Jet for modern thought by conceding that it was a funeral parlour and chapel of rest. A sign pointed to a veterinary surgeon's establishment (a converted shop) and another would-be modern vendor sold electrical equipment and 'pop' records.

Considerably heartened, Lisa came back the other side of the High Street and found a bus station and another little passage leading up a sharp slope to the railway station but, on investigation, Lisa discovered that it was little more than a halt, about to be closed soon because there were only two trains a day.

The bus station, on the other hand, was quite big, and there were two petrol stations, one with a workshop behind it. A bicycle shop attracted her and she promised herself a nice new bicycle, so that she could escape from this too-cosy inward looking town.

She went back to The Old House, without having seen the network of back streets that Queensmarket boasted, or the schools, the cottage hospital, the cluster of tiny factories and workshops, and so she was surprised to find that the shops were opening, and the surgery too, was on the point of opening. A queue of people had formed outside the gate, and they stared at her as she went in.

One of the men muttered to his neighbour; "Who's that, then?" and the other one growled, "That'll be his new one. Fancy him coming back here with her."

Lisa reddened but, when she looked back at them, they were staring woodenly ahead, patiently waiting for the door to open, at the side of the house; the side that wasn't connected to Martin Biddell's establishment.

Andrew met her on the way to open the door to the patients.

"Darling, where have you been? I wanted to speak to you before I opened surgery. Now it will have to wait until I come back from the rounds."

"I only went to look at the shops. Didn't Mrs. Tabb tell you?"

"Yes, but it shouldn't have taken an hour and a half should it? Just to walk round the Square?" Andrew protested. He had been worried about her continued absence, after the way he had been forced to neglect her last night, but his father had kept him talking, and he hadn't been able to get away in time before Lisa had fallen asleep.

"There are other shops," she pointed out gently. "I discovered the High Street."

"Oh." He looked uncomfortable. "Actually we don't go to the High Street. Mrs. Tabb thinks it's better to deal off our friends in the Square. Don't let her know."

"Andrew, don't go," Lisa urged. "There are so many things I want to ask you."

"Later, after surgery. Have you had any breakfast? Well, better get some. Mrs. Tabb has kept some hot for you but she doesn't like meals to be standing, so do try and be back in time for lunch, if you go out again."

"Can't I help you in surgery?" she asked forlornly, but he hadn't stopped to hear any more. With a general shake of the head for anything else she might suggest, Andrew withdrew into the surgery with as much finality as if he had stepped on to one of those two daily trains and gone to John o'Groats, she felt.

Mrs. Tabb was inclined to be rather frosty about the breakfast. "It's spoiled. Not fit for a dog to eat."

"I'm sorry," Lisa said contritely. "I tell you what – don't bother about cooking for me. Let me get my own food if I'm late back. Better still, I'll do the cooking for you!"

Mrs. Tabb whirled round.

"No, Miss Lisa – let it be understood

now and for all time, while there's breath in my body I do the cooking in this house. And I don't want anyone else in my kitchen."

"Not ever? What about your day off?" Lisa asked, again reddening.

"What would I want with a day off? Two hours I take off, between lunch and tea, twice a week, and I go to prayer meeting at the chapel on Sunday evening, but then I leave a cold supper laid in the dining-room and coffee in the percolator, and I wash up myself when I come back. Let's understand ourselves at the beginning, my dear, then we won't have any unpleasantness. I'm sure we can all get along together very nicely."

"Well, what *can* I do to help you?"

"Not a thing! It's not for the lady of the house to soil her hands. That's the way I was brought up. The way the women of this house have been brought up."

"Well, I must have something to do. Perhaps Andrew would let me do the accounts and send out the bills."

"Don't you go suggesting any such thing, my dear, or you'll have the old doctor after you. He's earmarked that little job for himself, so he won't be without a hand in the practice," Mrs. Tabb told her firmly. "Why don't you go and see the vicar?"

"Won't he come and see me?" Lisa asked.

"No, he won't come here." Mrs. Tabb chuckled. "Not after the high words he and the doctor nearly had over that last game of chess. Oh, sooner or later the old doctor will stump over to the vicarage and shout, 'Now see here, Hulbert, I was wrong over that last chess game but you should have borne with me, on account of your calling' and the vicar will say, 'Bless me, Bernard, if you'd given me a chance, I'd have been over to you first, but I was selecting the best moment to approach you'."

"Do they really go on like that?" Lisa asked, scandalised.

"Oh, yes, very close friends the old doctor and the vicar are," Mrs. Tabb said calmly. "They understand each other. And if I presume to say, Miss Lisa, you'd do better to take the old doctor in his stride rather than to look like a little scared rabbit at him. Never did I meet a man who was so much louder in his bark than in his bite. Stand up to him, my dear, and he'll like you better."

Lisa looked unimpressed, but she finished her breakast and automatically took the plates over to the sink.

"No! What did I say?" Mrs. Tabb reminded her.

"But I can't be lazy, Mrs. Tabb."

"You just take yourself over to the vicarage like I said. The vicar's daughter, Hazel, is about your age and you should get along fine together. There's embroidery and mother's meetings and doing the flowers and helping with the Sale of Work and opening bazaars – oh, you'll be so busy you'll wonder where half the day goes while you're not looking."

Lisa went upstairs and changed into something more suitable for a visit to the vicarage and went into the rain again, but she got no answer to her pealing on the old-fashioned bell rope of St. Anne's. Puzzled, she was about to walk away when the butcher's boy came from round the back of the house.

"No-one in," he said cheerily. "Found the order where she leaves it when she has to go out in a hurry. No good your waiting, missus."

No-one in at the vicarage. Nothing to do in The Old House. No music pupils and she was pretty sure that there was no room for music in the doctor's house. She hadn't even been shown all over it yet so she didn't know about the grand piano.

Lisa wandered disconsolately back to the Square, but now the shops were open and wore a different look. The antique shop in the corner attracted her. In the window was a very old mandolin, complete with ribbons. She stared at it with such longing that she didn't notice the proprietor come out.

"It is a very fine mandolin," he said experimentally.

She raised her eyes to his. He had a long thin dark face and his lank dark hair was streaked with grey. He had been a refugee from Central Europe some thirty years ago and was now reluctant to leave the refuge he had found in Queensmarket. This corner of the square was home, but the sad longing in Lisa's eyes for all she had suddenly lost, smote at him, reminding him of things better forgotten.

"You like music?" he said softly.

The word 'music' brought life leaping to those brown eyes of hers. She looked up at the top of the shop. 'Zilliachus Denner, Antiques' the name board said.

"Are you Mr. Denner?" she asked him.

He nodded.

"I've left my music behind me and there's nothing to take its place in The Old House," she found herself saying.

"The Old House?" His own dark eyes left her face and sought the flat white front of the doctor's house on the far side of the Square. "You are the young doctor's new wife?"

"Yes, I'm Lisa Lee," she replied, and held out her hand to him. Andrew had referred to these people as 'their friends in the Square' so there seemed nothing wrong in the little act.

It touched Zillie Denner. He stared at her hand, with its long sensitive fingers innocent of nail lacquer, hands so different from the beautiful yet destructive white ones he was thinking of at that moment. Then he took it in his and said, "You come into my shop, eh, and tell Zillie Denner all about it."

5

HE made some hot chocolate. It was in old-fashioned tall pottery beakers, each one with a queer gnome's face on it. Lisa traced the bumps of the features in the pottery with an exploring forefinger, and sipped the hot liquid with the frothy top, and felt better.

"You have a cream bun with it, no?" he tempted her, but Lisa shook her head. "I've just had a late breakfast and got into trouble about it," she smiled.

"It is your first day here," he said. He knew, of course, when she had arrived. They would all know, in this square.

She nodded.

He said carefully, clearing a space for himself to sit, on the end of a magnificent old carved chest, "We all heard about Dr. Andrew's marriage." Lisa felt that he had, with great restraint, avoided saying 'second marriage' and she felt the prick of uneasiness again.

"You don't have to be tactful with me,"

she said quickly. “I’m only too well aware by now of what it feels like to be the second wife.”

His dark eyes were inscrutable. “But you are happy, no?”

“Happy? What’s being happy?” she asked, with a frown. “I thought I knew, before I met Andrew.”

“Tell me what that happy time was like,” Zillie invited her, and she found she could talk easily to him and it came out with a rush. There wasn’t much to tell, of course. Just a simple, rather lonely life, with a little house that belonged to her, security with a smallish legacy in the bank and the money from her music pupils. Security in the knowledge that all the neighbours knew her, living as she did in a quiet London suburban street that had come to be her home, and all her pupils liked her. She had, too, her music. Her own piano . . .

“I didn’t know it then but, although I was lonely, there were no ghosts,” she found herself saying. “Funny, not long ago I wouldn’t have mentioned the word ‘ghosts’. I would have thought I was the most unimaginative, practical person.”

"With those hands? And that sensitive face? No, indeed no," Zillie said. "I understand about music, and what it feels, but there is the piano at The Old House."

"Is there?" It popped out before she could stop it. He looked so surprised that she didn't know, that she rushed on to say, "Well, of course, we only arrived late last night, and no-one had time to show me around and Mrs. Tabb made it clear that she didn't want domestic help, so I went out for a walk to explore. Andrew doesn't want help in the surgery and I've lost my pupils." She spread her hands. "Do you know, this is the frightening thing about it – I've got nothing to do and I'm not used to it. And no-one wants me," she finished, in a small voice that cut him to the heart.

"No! Not true! Everyone has someone who wants them. People are closely knit. If they think otherwise then they are either blind or stupid. No person is quite alone."

His vehemence embarrassed her. "What must you think of me for talking to you like this – a compete stranger? Anyone would think I wasn't happily married, but I am! I adore Andrew." She was only too miserably aware that she couldn't add with equal truth and vehemence that Andrew adored her also.

"I am not a stranger, I hope," Zillie Denner said, earnestly. "I have known the good doctor and his family for many years. I knew also the old doctor's father, for a short while, before he died. There has always been a Dr. Lee in that house. You should be proud to be one of the family."

"You *knew* the family? The other boys – Quentin and Tobias? Tell me about them!" she said eagerly.

Zillie's dark eyes clouded, and he appeared to hesitate but, whether because of a customer who came in at that moment, or from some other cause, Lisa couldn't say.

He excused himself and went into the shop.

She finished her chocolate, and looked round at the interesting things there but, when she couldn't decently hang around any longer, she threaded her way through to where Zillie was showing the customer a small convex mirror, and said goodbye and she would no doubt see him again.

"Goodbye, Frau Dokter," Zillie said absently. "Come again, sometime." Then recalling himself, he called, "I too, have a fine piano."

The bait. A piano. Of course she would be back. She waved and smiled. "Thank you!" she called and let herself out with a clanging of the shop bell.

But she felt better. She had found a friend.

She stood in the square, thinking. A clock tolled the hour with a dismal bell. That would be the church clock on the top of St. Anne's. Still a long time to kill, and she didn't want to go too far away. She had it in mind to hang about until Andrew came out to go on his rounds, and to ask him to take her with him. They might talk together in privacy, or at least she could be with him.

She suddenly ached to be with him, alone; without all these people who had prior claims on him.

She felt a little rush of jealousy that they should have known him for those early years of his life. She would have given the world to be able to look at a moving picture of him as a boy, and to see him perhaps swimming, fishing, skating, handling a boat. He must be able to do all those things, of course, coming from a place like this. But, she reminded herself, she knew very little of his pursuits and interests. She had known him such a short while and all they had done while courting had been to see films and shows, to go to dinners and concerts, and to discuss their present life. Their whole courtship had been based on the present, as if he had been afraid even to look back at the past . . .

She drew a deep breath. Be fair, she cautioned herself. He had talked to her a lot about his work in the path. lab., and of his ambitions for the future. He had discussed herself, listened to her talking about her family, her music, all the things that were dear to her heart. And, although she was well aware that he hadn't a clue about music, he had taken her to an awful lot of concerts and sat through them with apparent rapt attention. And he hadn't appeared to be holding back anything. But somehow he hadn't just given her much information about those previous thirty-five years.

Martin Biddell. She had to meet him sooner or later and she did need some things in the chemists. It would be a good place to keep watch for Andrew coming out, too.

Martin Biddell was the same age as Andrew, as tall and dark as Andrew, but without Andrew's distinguished good looks. Martin wore glasses and had a homely look, but Lisa liked him at once.

He came out from behind his counter, spick and span in his starched white coat, and took her hand in a hearty grip.

"It's Mrs. Andrew – I am glad to meet you. I was going to pop in this evening – didn't come last night. I thought you'd both like to settle in first. What a little thing you are!" and his eyes twinkled kindly down at her.

So, she told herself quickly, the other one must have been tall. Now she was beginning to think of that shadowy creature as a person, a shadow being gradually clothed with the facts she was gleaning. A person who had flung a very black shadow before she had died, making her mark on everyone who had known her – and she had been tall.

"I actually only dropped in for something to put on my face," Lisa said hurriedly. "I went out early this morning and the salt air stung my skin. It hurts."

He looked at her skin closely. Soft and fine, with the minimum of make-up. There was that odd *remembering* look in his face that Zillie Denner had had when he had first seen her.

"I'll get you some lotion to put on and, if you like, I'll suggest new make-up for you. The air's a bit keen for a fine skin like yours. Of course, if Andrew's already prescribed, don't let me tread on anyone's toes."

Her brown eyes widened, "No, Andrew hasn't said anything. I don't usually use much make-up."

"No, I can see that," he said quickly, and as if sensing that she might be hurt at his words, he added, "Oh, heavens, I didn't mean it like it must have sounded. I was rather pleased, actually. I mean it's no business of mine, but I'm always bucked when I see a woman with a fine skin and no need to plaster this stuff all over it," and he waved a rather contemptuous hand at a glass case containing an expensive range of cosmetics.

He didn't need to tell her. That was the sort of thing the *other one* had used.

She smiled and nodded. "Yes, I'm afraid I feel like that as well. I know I ought to try and look nice for Andrew's sake but I never could get worked up about make-up. All my pocket money used to go in . . . other directions." She was thinking of all the sheet music she used to buy, but there wasn't much sense in plugging it. The Lees, it appeared, were a non-musical family, and if it were true that there was a grand piano in that room which she hadn't yet seen, it was rather odd that Andrew hadn't mentioned it. That was a thing she would have to find out about.

Martin came back from behind the door marked 'Dispensary' and handed her a bottle of cloudy looking pink stuff.

"Just make a friend of this and you won't be sorry. You don't want the sea air to ravage that lovely skin of yours. It never really gets right again, unless you leave the place. And I suppose you're not banking on leaving us – I mean, you'll be here for good, won't you? I know the old man wanted Andrew back for keeps."

For keeps. She shivered. He might want Andrew for keeps, but no-one had indicated that she was included in that sentiment. But she nodded, all the same, and smiled.

"Well, goodbye, Mrs. Andrew," Martin said cheerfully, plainly at a loss to know what to say to her. But he held out his hand very kindly.

"I'm Lisa," she said shyly. "Won't you call me that? I want to be friends with all Andrew's friends."

"My dear girl!" he protested. "You will be – and not only because of Andrew's popularity. I daresay you'll do very well on your own score."

He was very nice, she thought, vaguely comforted, as she left the shop. He hadn't any idea of what she was like, but he had managed to touch on just the note she had wanted. To be liked for herself alone. It never occurred to her that Martin Biddell, like Zillie Denner, had been pleasurably surprised with the first sight of that sensitive young face, that had no pretensions to beauty but was interesting, likeable, and moreover, filled with warmth. Once they could reach her, draw her out, both men felt that she was the sort of woman everyone would very soon grow to love. The sort of woman Andrew Lee needed for a wife.

The car was outside The Old House now and a glance at Lisa's watch assured her that Andrew should really be closing surgery.

Suddenly the front door opened and he hurtled out, bag in hand, tugging on his coat. He didn't see her at first.

"Andrew, may I come with you on your rounds?" she asked him.

"Good heavens, Lisa, what are you doing standing outside like this?" he exploded. "What? No — no, not this one, my dear. It's a horror — accident at Shapplegate's Farm. Go in and ask Mrs. Tabb for some coffee or something. I don't know when I'll be back."

He said all that as he got in, started up the car, and wound down the window. He looked preoccupied. He was off before she could say anything.

Breakfast. Hot chocolate. Coffee. What did they think she was? A child, to be given something to eat or drink to keep it out of mischief?

She took her face lotion into the house. Mrs. Tabb was cleaning the stair-carpet with a Dustette. The flex was all over the place so Lisa left her lotion on the hall table and went out.

This time she made her way to the other part of the town that lay on the far side of the square.

Here she had a pleasant surprise. The rain had stopped and a watery sun was breaking through, but it was becoming warmer, and it wasn't difficult to see that the other side of the church held the best property, the best part of the coast and, moreover, the park Andrew had mentioned.

She went and sat in one of the shelters and thought about the people she had met. How friendly were the Lees with the chemist? She couldn't really see Zillie Denner coming over to the Lee house but he, too, had said he was very friendly with them. The vicar, whom she had yet to meet, seemed to be on the friendliest terms but, so far, she had yet to meet a girl, someone of her own age. Someone who wouldn't keep reminding her of that other person who had once been so close to Andrew.

She sat thinking of that bedroom and she was determined to have it changed. Although it wasn't that other girl's bed, she didn't want her room, either, and everything in Lisa revolted at the same habit as that other girl, no doubt, had instituted. Lisa didn't believe for one moment that Andrew had been the one to decide on sleeping in that poky little dressing-room. It wasn't like him to want that sort of existence. It wasn't like the kind and affectionate young husband who had shared the big double bed in the front of that comfortable little house that now seemed a world away; No. 19. A house without a grand or an old established name.

The thought brought a lump into her throat. She was for a terrible moment shatteringly homesick. Then it passed, which was as well, for a young woman came and sat on the end of her seat, looked enquiringly at her, looked away again and then smiled broadly and spoke to her.

"I say, are you by any chance Mrs. Lee?"

Lisa admitted that she was and waited. It was as she had feared. In this small place where everyone knew everyone else, she was known to them all by sight already, and she herself hardly knew anyone.

The young woman said, "Oh, good, because I should have felt an awful fool if you hadn't been. I'm Hazel Edwards. I expect you've heard of me. My father's the vicar – St. Anne's, you know."

"Oh, how do you do, Miss Edwards," Lisa said, and held out her hand.

"Call me Hazel. Everyone else does. It's what comes of having been brought up in a place. Half the old dears remember me as having been a particularly tiresome brat with one hair-ribbon always missing, and I don't seem to be able to grow out of it. It's an awful nuisance, though, because among other things, I'm standing in for the organist who is also the choir-master, while he's in hospital. Heaven knows when he'll be back and I just can't manage the brats."

Lisa smiled in sympathy. "I know exactly how you feel. I've been teaching music to small boys."

"Yes, I know. Zillie Denner told me. I just saw him. He told me you'd been to see him."

"How did you know where I'd be – or was it by chance that you found me here?"

Hazel had the grace to blush.

"No, nothing happens by chance in this place. (You'll find out!) Martin Biddell told me you'd asked the doctor to take you with him on his rounds – he heard you. After that, you were seen to cross the square, and Johnny Fitch told me you'd come to the park."

"Who is Johnny Fitch?" Lisa asked, rather crossly, not liking to feel that she was going to be followed, as well as being treated as a stranger.

"One of the choirboys. He was sent by his mother to get his young sister back, and she was trotting after you because she does, you know, when someone takes her fancy. She's only three."

Lisa looked at her hands. "I didn't know that any small child was following me or I'd have spoken to her. I must have been miles away."

"Homesick?" Hazel suggested. "I know how you feel. The only time they tried to get me into trim and send me away to boarding-school I was so homesick that I couldn't eat and I got ill. They had to fetch me back again."

"I'll be all right when I get used to it," Lisa said. "I might not have noticed how much I was missing home, if I hadn't been deprived of anything to do. I'm used to being busy. Mrs. Tabb won't let me turn a hand to anything, and they didn't even tell me there was a piano there. If I could only practice."

"I suppose you can't play the organ?" Hazel murmured, wistfully.

6

NOW Lisa felt comfortable. Here was another woman of her own age, one that she felt she was going to like.

She went back with Hazel to the vicarage. Hazel was a plump jolly girl of indeterminate colouring but a wide friendly smile. She was tremendously popular in the district with young and old alike, because of her unaffected friendliness and helpfulness, but it was easy to see that she wouldn't have much influence over the choirboys. They would think she was good for a lark, and it would never occur to them to treat her as a person who would bring discipline with her.

"I know you said you'd had enough to eat and drink already," Hazel said, "but one can always do with a cup of tea, I think. I'll make one. No good asking our Mrs. Knox. She's deaf as a post, and stupid when she feels like it. Usually when you want her to do something. She's not bad on the whole, though, and I shouldn't grumble, because if I had to do the cleaning and cooking as well as everything else, I'd go potty. What about that organ? Want to have a look at it?"

"Look, I've only played for pleasure. I didn't have many lessons and those were only voluntary because we knew the local organist," Lisa protested.

"I don't believe that," Hazel said stoutly. "You just climb up into that seat and have a go. I'm fed-up with things as they are. I mean, bad enough with the choir singing out of tune and no organ at all. If someone was up there blotting out their giggling, it might help to restore things to normal."

Lisa complied because she was longing for music – music at any price. She didn't do so badly with the one or two hymns and voluntaries she tried, but both girls admitted that it wasn't a sparkling performance.

"Never mind, you'll improve as you go on," Hazel said stoutly. "Oh, I'm glad you've come, Lisa! You can't think! I was getting end-of-tetherish, what with one thing and another – you know what I mean? But of course, I wouldn't have gone away. How could I leave Daddy? I wish he'd marry again, then I could get away, but let's face it, who'd have him?"

"Hazel! I haven't met your father but . . . "

"That's it!" grinned the unrepentant Hazel. "You just wait till you do!" She sipped her tea, her eyes crinkled with laughter above the edge of the cup. "He's as bad as your father-in-law. They make a fine pair. No wonder they're such great friends."

"My father-in-law! Oh, I forgot about him. I wonder if I've done the right thing, agreeing to your plan to play the organ, without asking his permission."

"Is this something I don't know about, because by and large I should think you couldn't please him better than helping out at the vicarage. It's the last thing the – "

She broke off with the same confusion that the other people had shown, so Lisa guessed who she had been going to refer to.

"Andrew's first wife? Now don't you start evading the subject. Everyone begins to mention her, then shuts up. Why don't they tell me what she was like?"

"Well, actually I didn't know her very well. I was still away at school in her time," Hazel said, busying herself with pouring fresh tea, though Lisa was protesting hard that she didn't want any more.

"It would be better for me to know what she was like, than to have a shadow behind me that everyone else knew and I didn't. I know she was tall!"

Hazel's eyes widened. "How did you know that?"

"You don't think Andrew would have told me?" Lisa hazarded. This was the greatest puzzle of all, and yet, she supposed, Andrew would hardly think it good taste to talk of the first one to her.

"No, I don't," Hazel said grimly.

"Even if I asked him to?"

Hazel shook her head. "Well, I mean, you couldn't could you? It's hardly done. I should forget about it. I tell you what! When people in this town get used to you, they'll forget her, too. And that's a promise."

"How can you be so sure?"

"Because I think you're rather nice, and everyone will soon grow to like you."

"Oh, now don't be kind! I just couldn't bear that!" Lisa said quickly.

"What's the matter with you? It's the truth. I never bother to flatter people. I think we're going to be friends – that's if you can put up with me. And if I say what I think about you, then you can take it it's the truth and no nonsense. I say, are you in a row or something, over at The Old House?"

"What made you say that?" Lisa said quickly.

Hazel grinned. "Someone always is, at sometime or other. It's the old doctor, but don't take any notice of him. He always lays about him. But he doesn't mean a thing really. Actually he's a wonderful man – well, a wonderful G.P. – but I don't suppose it's any different really. What I mean is, you can get wonderful doctors in hospital but it isn't quite the same as a wonderful G.P. He's almost as good as a clergyman – you know what

I mean. Knowing the people and caring about their private problems as well as their ailments. That's old Dr. Lee. He knows everyone in this town, and though he loves to give people the impression that he hates the lot of them, it isn't true. Not at all. I know."

"Well, I'm glad you've told me, because I might just have been under a misapprehension. I don't know if you realise it, but I thought he was a poisonous old brute! The way he looked at me last night when I arrived — "

"That's it. He's never at his best at night-time, and he'd had another row with Daddy over Chess and anyway, you can't do better than to help us over here because that's another thing — old Dr. Lee can't stand people being idle. Oh, it's not a bit of good you trying to tell him that your Mrs. Tabb won't let you do anything! He'd up and say that she was the housekeeper and you should tell her what you want to do. I'd just like to see the woman who dared to tell your Mrs. Tabb where to get off! She's worse than ours, and that's saying something."

And Lisa found that Hazel had been

right. The air seemed to have cleared when she went back to The Old House. Old Dr. Lee was almost affable at lunch when she asked timidly if anyone minded her playing the organ.

"Good heavens, don't tell me that a daughter-in-law of mine is good at something!" he snorted, which, Lisa supposed, was as near as he could bring himself to giving approval or praise.

Andrew, though looking rather tired, smiled his appreciation. "Oh, good, Lisa, I'm glad you've made a friend of Hazel and found some music. Hazel's a nice girl. She'll take you around. I've been wondering all the morning how I could arrange something for you but that takes a load off my shoulders."

"And you won't die of shame when you hear me fumbling with the organ stops on Sunday?" Lisa smiled.

Andrew exchanged a quick glance with his father. "Well I shan't be there, my darling, shall I? I've got surgery and the morning rounds, and there's evening surgery and calls. You'll be spared my blushes," he said, smiling at her again.

Lisa plucked up her courage. "What

about you, Dr. Lee? Won't you be able to come and hear me play?"

He winced at her calling him "Dr. Lee" but he didn't suggest anything else. He glared at her and said, "I'm not well enough to go to church. Can't you see that, girl?" but he was well enough to drink port after his excellent lunch, Lisa couldn't help noticing, and well enough to go out for a short walk after lunch, leaning heavily on his sticks.

"Shall I walk with you?" she asked him, anxiously, but he didn't answer her, and Andrew frowned at her.

Still, it gave them a chance to be alone together, she thought, and the minute Andrew's father was out of the house, in the now warm sunshine, she threw herself at her husband.

"Andrew, there are such a lot of things I want to talk to you about, and this is the first time we've been alone since we left No. 19, yesterday!"

"I know, my dear, I know," he said, and briefly cuddled her. As an afterthought, it seemed, he kissed her, and perhaps because she was being rather observant and introspective, she fancied that his kiss was mechanical rather than affectionate.

"Andrew, first of all, our sleeping arrangements. I don't like them. You in that poky little dressing-room and me in that big room. I don't like it. Let's not."

"But Lisa, it was only for last night," he said, in some surprise. "You were tired out, and I couldn't think straight, what with one thing and another, and when I found you were fast asleep when I went upstairs, I was sure I'd done the right thing in allowing Mrs. Tabb to persuade me. She's a good soul. You can't do better than follow her advice."

Lisa let that last sentiment slide for the moment and tackled the more important point. "Andrew, she said it had always been like that. That it was your habit to sleep apart on account of the telephone calls in the night."

"Yes, well – " he began, looking uncomfortable.

Lisa fancied that he was about to tell her that in the old days it had worked out like that. She didn't want to know about the sleeping habits of her predecessor so she broke in swiftly, "Andrew, it won't disturb me, telephone calls and you putting the light on and getting up. I sleep like the dead."

"Lisa!" he protested, in a shock voice.

"Sorry! You know what I mean. Like a log, then. I shall be much less comfortable if I have to get used to sleeping alone. Goodness, I'm married to you. I want the comfort of being with you, don't I, and by the look of it, it doesn't appear that I shall get much of that in the daytime!"

"No, well, all right then, dearest, if that's what you want, you'd better arrange something else with Mrs. Tabb."

"There'll be an argument. Will you back me up if she comes to you?"

He looked distressed, impatient. "Well, if I must, but I've got more than enough on my hands at the moment."

"Sorry to bother you, darling, but I shall be all right if we can fix the sleeping arrangements."

"Oh, good, is that all, then, because I would like to read the newspaper. I never get a chance in this madhouse."

"You've only been here half a day. You don't know what it will be like," Lisa pointed out.

"Oh, don't I!" he said shortly.

"Yes, I forgot that you admitted to me yesterday that you'd been in practice with your father before. Why didn't you tell me about it, Andrew?"

"Really, Lisa, dear, I hardly thought you'd be interested. I suppose I just didn't think."

"Why did you break up the partnership and go back to the hospital?" she pressed.

He looked warily at her. She had never seen him look like that before. And then that fleeting expression had gone, and he smiled quite naturally and said, "It's no secret, my dear, that pathology was the one thing that interested me. As soon as I had a chance to get out of the partnership I did. My father was in good health in those days and very glad to have the place to himself, I've no doubt. Anyway, I was glad to get back to the hospital," and it struck Lisa that he almost but not quite permitted himself to add that he wished he was back there now.

She sighed. "Oh, then that's cleared up, though I can't think why you had to come back now. Not for always, I mean. Temporarily, I should have thought, till your father was well again. There doesn't seem much the matter with him — he's out walking now!"

"I know that, don't I, but it's one of his good days. I hear that he isn't always as well, and anyway, it's what he wants, and he isn't getting any younger. Now don't let's go over all that again, Lisa."

"Weren't the other sons doctors?" she thrust at him.

His head shot up. She had used shock tactics. She had meant to. And it had worked. He had a definite hunted look on his face. She stared at him fascinated.

"Oh, I suppose the local people have been talking to you, recounting family history," he said, with no great pleasure in his voice.

"No. They haven't. I got that out of Mrs. Tabb, by dragging it out of her. She reluctantly told me their names, after having given the subject due consideration and deciding at last that it couldn't possibly matter since I was sure to hear it some time or other from people around who knew them."

"So now you know, Lisa."

"Yes, now I know — that much. But it

isn't the point, Andrew! What I wanted was for you to tell me about it yourself, and a long time ago. Why didn't you tell me?"

"What could I have told you? How could I have been sure that the information would interest you? I did rather flatter myself that you were interested in me, not my family. I was – not exactly estranged from my family, but certainly not very close with them. Now may we drop it, Lisa?"

"No, Andrew, no we can't drop it. I want to know all about you. It isn't natural for me not to; in fact it's frankly embarrassing. I go about this town – your home – a complete stranger. People get to know me – they want to, because I belong to you – but they knew you and the rest of your family before you met me, and they think it quite natural to talk about your family and I feel a complete fool because I don't know a thing about them."

"Don't talk to people about the family, then. Surely there must be a lot of other things to discuss? The town's very interesting, and you know I don't mind you developing activities in connection with the church and the parish."

"You mean you're not going to tell me anything. There are things you don't want me to know."

"No, Lisa, no, no, it isn't like that at all! Look, my dear, it's just family history. I'm so used to it that it hardly occurred to me that you'd want to know about it, but as you do – you've expressed a wish to hear all about it – then let's give it a fair go, and leave it for a time when I can have no interruptions while I'm telling you all about it. Then you won't get the wrong idea."

"When will there be a time when there are no interruptions?" she asked him.

"I'm taking a day off next week," he said desperately and it occurred to her that he had only just thought of it. "Perhaps we would go somewhere for the day – a picnic or something – and then I'll tell you all about it. Meantime Lisa, please don't go around asking other people for information."

"I don't ask them! It comes out in conversation and I have to ask them what they mean," she said indignantly.

"Change the subject then, and let me be the one to give you my version first."

"Won't they think it a little odd that I don't know and won't let them talk about it?"

The telephone rang. He got up wearily to take the call. On his way to the instrument, he answered her question. "No, they won't think it odd," he told her flatly.

7

LISA settled down to being busy with her church activities after that. Secure in the knowledge that one day next week she would have a day out with Andrew, and that he had promised to tell her everything, she sunk herself in her music.

In the mornings she would drop in to Zillie Denner's to play his grand piano for an hour. This was at his suggestion, when he heard from Hazel that Lisa's afternoons and evenings and Sundays would all be taken up with the organ, until their organist came back.

"You don't know how much pleasure this gives me," he said one morning to Lisa, when she had finished playing some Beethoven he had chosen, and he had brought in the beakers of hot chocolate. "I have not heard such playing for oh, how long? Well, since my sister went back to our own country. Now I am alone and there is no-one to play. Well,

I have a radio, but what is radio, after listening to my own piano?"

There were mornings when he wanted only Bach, and there were times when he would say, "Now, Lisa child, play anything. Please yourself – play anything. I don't care!" and Lisa would roam through the tangle of pieces she liked best, from popular classics to folk tunes, bits of Highland reels and heart-tearing melodies from Ireland. Zillie would say it wasn't good music, but he liked it, all the same.

By tacit agreement they never mentioned the past, after Lisa had happened to mention that Andrew had promised to tell her all about it. Only once did Zillie make a slip, and mention something that gave her yet another clue to what Andrew's first wife had been like, and that was through the piano.

"It is a fine one, this piano of mine, but not as good as the one in The Old House. Many's the time I've tuned it, and caressed it. I got it for them, you know, from a good friend of mine. He didn't want to sell it but he needed the money, and they – well, *she* had to have what she wanted, and no argument. Oy, oy-oy, what a woman!"

Lisa held her breath, waiting to hear more, but Zillie stiffened, realising what he had said, so Lisa said casually, "Hasn't it been tuned since you last went over there, Zillie? That won't help it, will it?"

"No, it will not help it," he said, tight-lipped.

"Mrs. Tabb polishes the outside of it, every day. I've seen her, once, when the door was opened," Lisa offered, watching him, but he wouldn't rise to the bait any more. He merely grunted.

She liked her mornings with him but best of all she enjoyed her afternoons with Hazel. Hazel was a wonderful person for making every hour sheer enjoyment. Even if it was only sitting together mending the tattered hymn books, or turning out one of her drawers, it was all good fun.

"Are you missing your piano pupils?" she wanted to know, one afternoon, as they sat eating Mrs. Knox's seedy cake and cherry biscuits, and trying to work out how to fit in the decorating of the stalls for the next Bring and Buy Sale and advance marshalling of helpers for the Garden Party.

"Yes, more than I thought possible," Lisa sighed. She had plenty of time to miss them. Although Andrew had agreed to different sleeping arrangements, Mrs. Tabb had been an unexpected obstruction, declaring that she couldn't get the only other available room ready yet, as it had to be re-decorated, and she had her hands too full to settle them in there and have to have them out again for the decorators to come in. During the long sleepless nights Lisa would go over again the time of her brief marriage, remembering the full and happy days with her pupils, and the secure and comfortable nights with Andrew. Now both had been taken away from her and she felt curiously empty.

"Well, I don't know how you feel about it, but Mrs. Pendleton's fallen out with Amy Clickett – she wasn't much good anyway, I have to admit, and the Pendleton child's a perfect bind, but if you could see your way to take the brat over, it would win Mrs. Pendleton round to helping me with the cake stall. She really is a wonderful cook, and she isn't short of money."

"I wonder you haven't the grace to blush!" Lisa exclaimed. "Of all the barefaced manoeuvring – !"

Hazel chuckled. "Ah, go on! What do you care? You'll be getting the chance to teach. I bet that's all you like about it – the teaching, not the brat itself. Anyway, if you were a vicar's daughter, you'd do just the same as I do. Ways and means, that's the dictum of every day, and if you'll believe me, it gets so that one just doesn't care what one proposes so that everything works out more or less without a hitch. I find myself roping in the most unlikely people to do things."

"I can imagine," Lisa murmured, then they both laughed. "All right, though wait a minute – if I say I'll teach the Pendleton child, what do I do for a piano?"

"Go to the Pendleton house, of course. The mother likes her little dear to keep to their own piano, and incidentally to sit in the next room and hear what she's getting for her money."

"Then that's all right," Lisa said.

"Because if you were going to mention that grand piano in our house, which is kept locked, I should scream."

Hazel blinked, but refused to be tempted into commenting on that. She said instead, "The Pendleton house is on the road to Pondersfield Green. Do you drive?"

"No, and I wouldn't be allowed to have the car anyway. A doctor's car is sacred."

"I thought you might be given one of your own."

Hazel looked sorry the moment she had said it, and Lisa thought she knew why.

She sighed. What if the first Mrs. Lee had had a car of her own? If someone bought Lisa one, it was doubtful if she would be able to drive it without running into trouble, she told herself crossly.

"I daresay I can borrow a bike," she said.

"I wouldn't. That road isn't much good for cyclists. I'll drive you over if you like, and pick you up again, though there is a bus of sorts. You have to check the time carefully, and the buses are a law unto themselves. They might get there five minutes early or late, whichever way the wind blew them."

"I'll take a bus. You haven't got any time to drive me about," Lisa said firmly. "You never know – Andrew might be able to take me."

Lisa was out of the house a lot, one way and another, but no-one seemed to miss her.

Andrew was out of the house, or in surgery, most of the time, so he rarely knew where she was. Mrs. Tabb didn't care so long as Lisa was in early to meals. The old doctor was just as glad if he didn't have to see her at all.

At first Lisa told herself she was imagining things, but there was one day when they came face to face. She had been hurrying down the stairs as he came out of his room and they stood staring into each other's eyes for a full minute. From sheer embarrassment, Lisa flashed him that brilliant smile of hers and said a nervous, "Hello!"

She didn't quite know what she expected of him, but certainly not what she got. He looked at her with sheer distaste, and growled, "You're too young to be a doctor's wife. Why don't you go to a hairdresser, put some stuff on your face – or whatever women do to look older."

She whitened, her smile vanishing. Nervously she pushed back her soft brown hair, and into those brown eyes of hers a hurt look came that was to worry old Dr. Lee for days. She slid past him with a muttered apology and ran out of the house.

Not even her organ practice in the silent, empty church, could ease the pain that her position began to bring. Unwanted, quite unnecessary in the scheme of things at The Old House, she wondered how long she could bear it. She promised herself that whatever Andrew had to tell her on that day off of his, she would go back to London for a short while; take time off to think, consider her position and whether she would return. After all, they hadn't heard yet that Mrs. Cobb had had her passage settled, to go to Australia. It might be as well to see what she was doing about things, and if she were going to leave soon, to settle a new person into the house.

Lisa was so glad that that house of hers hadn't been sold. It was so comforting to know that at least she owned a roof over her head. It was at that point that she recalled that Andrew had said she could stay there if she liked, and he would come to her at the week-ends. At this stage it seemed a much more preferable arrangement, and she wondered if he had known how it would be in Queensmarket and had tried to save her from the treatment she was receiving in his own home.

Still, she had come with him and it was useless to speculate on how it would have been if she hadn't. She could of course have kept her own piano pupils, but what would the neighbours have said about her new husband leaving her? She sighed. Either way it seemed to be fraught with difficulties, and she would just have to make the best of it.

She had been thinking of all this and playing the organ without really watching what she was doing.

A voice called her back to herself and she saw the vicar standing looking up at her.

"That was very nice, my dear," he remarked.

"Oh, was it, vicar? I'm afraid I was day-dreaming," she confessed. She liked him and wondered how he managed to get on with her father-in-law at all, because he seemed rather an easy-going man. He was short and plump, with a rather fleshy, heavily jowled face and sloping-shaped eyes that rather reminded her of a sad-looking spaniel. An odd choice of friend for old Dr. Lee. She supposed it was because of their mutual love of Chess.

"My daughter Hazel tells me you're prepared to go on doing this until our organist comes back," the vicar said, as she joined him in the chancel. "It's really very good of you, and if you have any more spare time I was wondering whether you would do something else to help the poor fellow."

Lisa was surprised. Didn't he know it wasn't to help the organist, whom she didn't know, but to help the overworked Hazel?

"What is it?" she asked cautiously.

"He hasn't anyone to go and see him," the vicar said hesitantly. "I go when I can, and my daughter, of course, but she doesn't seem to get on very well with him. I can't think why. He seems to me a very pleasant chap. Would *you* go and visit him once in a while, I wonder?"

"Well, I'd like to help, vicar, but if I'm to practise in the evenings, it won't give me much chance."

"I was thinking of the mid-week visiting hour which is in the afternoon," the vicar said mildly.

"If it doesn't clash with Andrew's one day off, I'd like to help you," she said, at last, because the vicar's sad-dog face wasn't really giving her much chance to get out of it.

Her duties began to mount up. Primarily because she liked being with Hazel and helping her, Lisa found herself roped into all sorts of church activities. She found herself believing that all the women of the parish had been briefed not to mention Andrew's first wife, because they put on very bright smiles on first meeting her and telling her they were so glad to see her and to welcome her into their midst, but all the time they looked as if they were dying to say that she was so different, and they were also trying, not very successfully, to refrain from exchanging glances with each other.

Her ability to play both organ and piano assured her popularity, she found. The news of her taking over the Pendleton child brought her three other pupils, especially when it was learned that she had been to a school of music and had initials after her name – which the luckless Amy Clickett hadn't.

Lisa went specially to see Amy Clickett to explain to her that she hadn't any wish to take her pupils away from her, but she found Amy Clickett was already teaching in the day school and cheerfully said she would be glad to unload one or two more on Lisa, if she liked teaching the piano so much. She mentioned one or two children who sounded as if they might be too unruly for anyone's taste.

Lisa forgot about the promised visit to the organist in hospital, because of what happened with her first visit to the Pendleton house.

It was a new house, smallish and ornate. Mrs. Pendleton, Lisa found, was very much like her house. A social climber, she gushed over Lisa, mentioned her degree and told her a great deal about Patricia, who was nine.

Lisa could see all that was untrue at a glance, but interpreted it in a different way. Patricia would have no talent at all for playing the piano, and anyway, the child was bored and rather insolent.

When they had been left alone together, Lisa said, "I don't suppose you really want to go on learning out of this book, do you?"

Patricia stared distastefully at the manual she had laboriously ploughed through the first ten pages of, in two years, and her pleasure at the thought of abandoning it, warred with her suspicion. "Why are you letting me off it?" she asked.

"I never believe in teaching anyone from a book they don't like," Lisa said mildly. "Music isn't something to keep *going* at. It's a thing to be *enjoyed.*"

"I could manage to live without it," Patricia said pertly.

"I was just wondering if you'd like to learn a piece right off, this evening, so you could show off at the next party you go to. Not any old piece, but a smart modern number."

It was heavy going, combating Mrs. Pendleton who kept popping in to see why no scales were being played, and the child's distressing mood. Patricia would have loved to learn a number in one evening, to swank with it to her friends, but she had neither the agility of fingering nor the mental processes to learn the notes, and she quickly lost her temper when she found she couldn't do it.

Lisa worked overtime on the child, and managed some sort of result to the satisfaction of both Patricia and her mother.

"But this is marvellous! The other stupid woman couldn't get poor Patricia beyond ten miserable pages of elementary primer!"

"Don't blame her previous teacher. We all have our different methods. I personally employ a different technique to suit each pupil," Lisa said quickly, not wishing to undo the cordial atmosphere existing between herself and Amy Clickett. In this new life she couldn't afford to upset anyone.

Mrs. Pendleton took it to mean that Lisa was a superior sort of teacher who naturally employed different methods to one as lowly as Amy Clickett. Gushing and beaming, she said to Lisa, "Where did you park your car? I'll walk you out to it."

"I haven't got a car. I shall catch a bus, if I can," Lisa said, hating the thought of such an admission to this woman.

"Nonsense. I shall go and fetch my husband to drive you home, Mrs. Lee."

"Daddy's still got his visitor with him," Patricia pointed out.

"Then I shall interrupt him. It's only that Mr. Mawson. Who does he think he is, staying all this time as if he had been invited? He only came about the pedigree puppy we're having from him. The idea!"

Mawson. The name rang a bell. Lisa looked at Patricia who had stayed with her.

"Who is this Mr. Mawson? I think I might know him."

Patricia looked slant-eyed at her. "I shouldn't think you would want to know him," she said. "He's just a farmer. They used to be rich but not any more. That's why Mummy doesn't want him to be a visitor here."

Now Lisa placed him. Carmichael Mawson. Old friend of the Lees, whose family had now all gone. He had been at school with Andrew. Andrew had mentioned him, when he had been trying to paint an attractive picture of his home town, Lisa remembered.

Mrs. Pendleton came back, two men at her heels. She looked offended. "Our visitor seems to want to drive you back in his shooting brake," she said, with distaste.

Carmichael Mawson came towards Lisa, holding out his hand. "May I take you home, Mrs. Lee? I've been wanting to meet you. Your husband . . . was an old friend of mine."

8

CARMICHAEL MAWSON was as tall as Andrew, and big built. His tweeds smelt of tobacco smoke, and the farm; a queer, not unpleasant earthy, masculine smell, the good healthy odour of a man who lives his life among animals in the open air. He strode beside her, pleasantly chatting, until they reached his shooting brake, which, Lisa saw, absolutely matched his own appearance. Good, solid, yet well-worn.

Of course, it was hardly surprising that Patricia's mother didn't want him as a visitor. She probably had brocade furniture in her drawing-room, and would hardly relish a suit that had come straight from the farmyard, embellishing her spotless armchairs.

Carmichael Mawson opened the door for Lisa. He hadn't bothered to lock the brake. He wouldn't, she thought. The seats were leather, slashed and scraped here and there. Probably he brought his dogs with him usually, and they were no respecters of upholstery.

"You know," he confided, as he started up the brake and edged carefully out into the busy road, "I don't know quite what I expected; you are a complete surprise to me."

"Why? Didn't Andrew tell you what I looked like?"

"Andrew, my dear girl, has no great gift for describing people. Describing wounds and germs and new discoveries in his laboratory, yes; people – no!"

"Well, didn't you see our wedding picture in the Press?"

"I saw one picture – it was enough for me," he said, vigorously. "I didn't bother to find any others. That picture! Did you see it, I wonder? Andrew looking faintly astonished, crowds of people (presumably from his hospital) laughing idiot fashion (at what, I couldn't see!) and the bride, bent almost double in her efforts to avoid the shower of rice and confetti so that I couldn't decide on her height at all. Her colouring was also lost because of a silly flowered hat with a veil that blew everywhere, and she was screwing her face up."

"Oh, dear. I see what you mean, Mr. Mawson."

"Carmichael, m'dear. I'm an old friend of your husband's and I hope I may call you Lisa. And never fear – you are an immense improvement on your picture in the newspaper."

"Thank goodness for that," Lisa chuckled. She liked him. He was just the sort of best friend that Andrew would have! "I'm so glad I've met you in this nice way. When are you coming to see us?"

He didn't answer that at once. Instead, he asked her, "Have you settled into The Old House yet?"

"Settled! That's an odd expression. If you mean have I been permitted to enter it, yes, I have – just about. But no-one lets me do anything. Life, I imagine, goes on just the same as before I came. Mrs. Tabb won't let me touch a thing. She just shoos me out as if I were a child."

"Oh, Mrs. Tabb. Yes, she's one of the band of faithful. We've got one – Mrs. Reckless. Not a bit like her name, of course – just the opposite, in fact, and

I don't believe she's ever really been married. She carries on the tradition of the old biddies, but the salt of the earth, of course. But if I ever married, the poor girl would have an awful time, because d'you see, Mrs. Reckless has been boss of the show all this time, and that's what she likes best. The same with your Mrs. Tabb – and of course, the redoubtable Mrs. Knox at the vicarage. You know Hazel, of course?"

Lisa admitted that she did, and liked her.

"Yes, nice girl. Does she mention the organist?" he asked unaccountably.

"Many times. She's persuaded me to take his place until he comes out of hospital, though I don't think anyone has told me what he's in there for. Was it an accident?"

"You'd better ask Hazel," he said. "Now, how *is* old Andrew? I spoke to him over the telephone and he sounded very fit."

"He's well, but tired. General practice isn't like the peaceful life he had in the path. lab. of his old hospital," Lisa said slowly.

"Ah, well, he knew what he was letting himself in for, of course," Carmichael said. "Do you like Queensmarket?"

"It's an interesting place," Lisa allowed. "Of course, I haven't seen much of it yet. Hazel keeps me pretty busy, but of course I'd rather have it that way."

"Have you made any friends in the square? You're the music lover, aren't you? Have you met Zillie Denner?"

"Yes. Hasn't he told you?" Lisa laughed. "Everyone seems to know about everybody else here."

"I'm rather isolated, up at the farm," Carmichael told her. Again she was conscious of a restraint somewhere but couldn't imagine what had provoked it. Something she had said? Something to do with Zillie Denner?

"I go and play for Zillie in the mornings sometimes. He has a fine grand piano, but not, he assures me, so fine as the one at The Old House," and she waited, with baited breath. What could Carmichael have to say about that?

He drove on in silence, so she said, "I suppose you play, too?"

"Oh, no, indeed. I can't tell one note

from another. It's kind of you to play for Zillie, though. I expect he misses his sister."

"Yes, he told me he did. And of course, now I'm trying to teach young Patricia to play — "

That did raise a spark in him. "Oh, that awful child! That awful family! What made you?"

Lisa told him how it had come about. "I don't really mind. I'd hate to give up teaching music altogether."

"You like children?" he asked.

"Oh, yes, very much," she said warmly. "I think a house without children — " and she broke off, for suddenly that was what was wrong with The Old House, and so far as she could see, neither Andrew nor his father had any use for children around. She swallowed on the lump in her throat and said again, "It's very kind of you to bring me home, and I've so much enjoyed meeting you. Will you come and see us at The Old House?"

He edged the brake into the square, on Zillie's corner. "I'll stay here, if you don't mind. It's easier to get out again," he explained, though Lisa couldn't see how that came about. "And regarding visiting, to be honest, I don't get much chance. I have to be at the farm all the time, but that's no reason why you shouldn't come and visit us. Mrs. Reckless would love to have you. She likes children, too – there are several in and out of the place, mostly belonging to the farm workers. They help around the stables, or just get in the way."

"I'd like that, very much!" Lisa told him.

"Then you do that. Any time – don't bother to let us know. And if you feel you could knock out a tune on our harmonium, Mrs. Reckless would adore you! No-one ever does that for her, and the old harmonium is her greatest treasure."

"Are you sure it wouldn't bother you? People who don't understand music don't usually – well, of course, Dr. Lee isn't well and – " Lisa floundered hopelessly. She had given away the situation at home and she hadn't meant to.

He looked angry, in the light from the street lamp. "They should have given away Tressida's piano if they didn't want anyone else to touch it," he muttered.

Tressida. So that was her name. Lisa was trembling, without quite knowing why. The name – unusual enough in all conscience – somehow fitted the picture of that dead girl that she was building up in her mind.

But before she could ask him about Tressida Lee, he was talking smoothly about how she could get to the farm. "Elmgates is high on the hill. You can't miss it. Do you drive, Lisa? No, well, never mind, there's a bus of sorts that goes to the crossroads – you can't miss the ones I mean. They point to Skegwell, Pondersfield Green, Chipping Bridge and Monks Rawley respectively. Get out of the bus at the crossroads and take the road marked Chipping Bridge, and you'll see a lane branching off it to the right. You walk up it for two miles, and if you're not dropping at the end of it, you'll see a footpath. We're at the end of the footpath."

"At the end of a footpath?" Lisa asked incredulously, not quite sure if he was being serious.

"Well, yes, that's for people on foot.

It's a short cut. There's a lane of sorts leading up from the top of the road for vehicles. Don't forget to shut the gates, will you, and don't let Tinker frighten you. His bark is worse than his bite."

"What is Tinker?"

"Collie. Do you like dogs?"

"Yes, I love animals. All small things." She sighed. "I must go now. I wish you'd come in and see Andrew and his father, though. You could have, without losing time – the hours we must have been sitting here talking."

"Go on, Andrew wouldn't want to see me at this time of night, that's if he's in, of course."

"He never was like that, not in London," Lisa said. "Carmichael, before you go, I have a favour to ask you. No-one will mention his first wife to me. You haven't. You've talked of everything else and everyone else, but not her. Except to mention her name, and I didn't even know that."

"It's all past, Lisa. Let it rest. Think of the future with Andrew. He chose you. You remember that."

"Yes, but why did he? I mean, what was *she* like? Am I like her, or so different that I don't remind him of her?"

"Oh, Lisa, don't start thinking on those lines. You're way off the beam," he protested.

"But what *was* she like? I know she was tall – it slipped out when someone was talking. So I'm the exact opposite. I'm pretty certain she wasn't my colouring, either. That's true, isn't it?"

"Yes, that's true," he said, in a muffled voice.

"Tell me, what was she *like*?"

"Lisa, I can't tell you what she was like. I haven't any words to describe her," he said desperately. "There just wasn't anyone quite like her. There, does that answer your question?"

"Yes, I think so," she said doubtfully. "Thanks for telling me that much."

He got out of the car hastily and caught at her hand. "No, don't go off like that. I've given you the wrong impression, I know I have. That's why I avoided speaking of her. I was pretty sure Andrew wouldn't have mentioned her to you, and for the same reason you won't get anyone else to. If only you hadn't wanted to *know*."

"Well, how am I supposed to feel?" she choked. "When we were in London, Andrew and I, we were so happy together that I hardly ever thought of the fact that I was only the second wife. It didn't seem to matter there. But it does here — terribly! In so many ways. People want to see me, to compare me with her, I know they do! And they look surprised, so isn't it natural that I should want to know why? I want to look into their minds, see a picture of her, how she looked and walked and talked, how she treated Andrew and how . . . how he treated her."

"Don't," Carmichael said. "I've only met you tonight, and I like you already, and I don't want you to think like that. You're all wrong about it, I assure you."

"Oh, am I? You wouldn't say that if you could see how old Dr. Lee looks at me," she said, in a low voice.

"Well, that's a different story," he retorted.

"Then tell me about that story – I have a right to know why, haven't I?"

"Yes, but not from me. Least of all from me."

"Who, then? Who, Carmichael?"

"Andrew!" he said fiercely.

"Yes, I suppose you're right. Actually I have asked him and he has said he'll tell me all about everything on his day off next week."

"There you are, then!"

"But what does he call 'all about it'? What does he consider is 'everything'? I bet he'll omit to tell me the things I really want to know, not because he's going to be dishonest about it but because he'll believe I ought not to know. He's protective of me, in an odd sort of way that keeps on reminding me that he's so much older than I am. I wish he wouldn't. Was *she* his age?"

"There you go again. Pandora, that's you! Do you know what happened to Pandora, Lisa?"

"Of course I do, but there's no comparison! She was just wilfully inquisitive. I'm wanting to know what happened before. Every wife does, whether she's the second, or the first, and husbands usually make their lives an open book to their new wives."

"Oh, do they!" he said shortly, and laughed.

"You're deliberately misconstruing what I meant," she told him severely. "I didn't mean it like that — I meant an open book regarding their relatives and the ordinary things they have done in their lives. Bless me, I didn't even know that Andrew wasn't an only child until the other day when someone told me about Quentin and Tobias."

"It hasn't been a happy household, Lisa," he said quietly. "One day you'll understand why poor old Andrew has appeared to be reticent about some things."

"But not to *me*, his wife?" she burst out. "It makes me think I can't be trusted, what with one thing and another. And don't think I'm going around talking like this to everyone. I'm not. But you're his great friend, and you knew them all so well and I feel I can talk to you like this."

"I'm deeply honoured, Lisa, and I wish I could do something for you, but I can't. Except to remind you that *she* was what he wanted then but *you* are the best for him now."

9

LISA didn't realise it but she was now living for that day which Andrew had promised her.

Every morning she sat facing him at breakfast, and felt miles apart. He buried himself behind his newspaper because it was the only chance he got to read it, so Lisa had no conversation with him. Mrs. Tabb chose his breakfasts and poured his coffee for him, taking away what Lisa had once enjoyed as the greatest pleasure in a wife's life. Those breakfasts in London had been fun; intimate, cosy, jolly.

These breakfasts were Mrs. Tabb-ish, Lisa thought resentfully. At The Old House there was a huge round table in the breakfast-room, and the cloth was 'saved' by huge white place mats, plain and utilitarian, a warning to the breakfasters not to spill anything. The silverware was all highly polished, and the china was part of the big set that had come to The Old

House with Andrew's great-grandmother. Mrs. Tabb had told Lisa that so severely that Lisa felt she was suspected of being capable of breaking pieces of it.

"It can't be matched," Mrs. Tabb had told her with satisfaction, and Lisa thought wistfully of the breakfast set she and Andrew had started their married life on – each piece a bright and daring colour, easy to replace if an accident happened, and somehow a heart-lightener on a grey morning to see tea or coffee in scarlet or sunshine yellow pottery.

Little things, but what a big part they played in a life, Lisa thought miserably. Even the food Andrew ate was different. In London he had had cereals from gay packets, followed by grilled bacon, and marmalade bought from the shop round the corner, and together they read out all about the free gifts each had to offer.

In Queensmarket he had porridge – unrelenting porridge followed by kidneys and bacon, or sausages slightly over done; the great egg-tray filled with medium boiled eggs which had to be eaten between Andrew and Lisa or Mrs. Tabb would be offended, and of course kippers and haddock. It seemed to Lisa that Andrew had tried to get as far from the old life in every respect as possible, and that now he was back here again Mrs. Tabb was deliberately following the old routine; the way things had been when that other one was alive. Sitting in Lisa's place at the table . . .

He looked up suddenly and smiled at her. Such a kind little smile. He said, "What are you thinking about?"

She couldn't say, "I'm thinking of how all this was, before you even met me," because it just wasn't done. But that was what she was trying to do; see the person who had been in that chair.

She shook herself, and leaving her chair, slid to the floor beside him and put her cheek on his arm. "Andrew, I love you so much," she choked, and buried her face against him.

"Don't, dearest, get up, do," he said, in a queer embarrassed voice, and when she wouldn't, he sat there rubbing the back of her head absently.

She got to her knees at last with a shaky laugh. "I hope you aren't going to become one of those husbands who feel their wives shouldn't display affection because they're married."

"What an involved remark!" he said. He took her face in his hands and studied it, trying to read those brown eyes, to see if anything had gone wrong. "Aren't you happy? But of course you are – you must be. You've got piano pupils again, and we're here together. It isn't as if I'd left you alone in London, all that way away."

He had answered himself, leaving her nothing to say. Settled it tidily, with them both in the same house and Lisa suitably occupied all day while he was up to his ears in the work of the practice. What could be wrong, he was asking himself.

"I'd like you to remember I'm here sometimes," she said shakily, "and that I'm not a child."

"Who said you were?" he said gently, laughing softly. "But of course you are, really, you know. Look at you, in that dress! Did you wear any different when you were fifteen?"

"It's supposed to be suitable for a doctor's wife in the mornings and it's called a silk poplin shirt-waister," she said, half indignant.

"Then I'm sure that if that's what it's called, it must be right," he chuckled, and kissing the top of her head, he left the breakfast table, and the room . . . her life, Lisa thought, resentfully, listening to his retreating footsteps towards the surgery. He would be in that room on the other side of the tiled hall, for most of the morning, yet he might just as well have been in London, she felt he was so far apart from her.

Mrs. Tabb came in to clear the table. Desperately Lisa stood up in front of her and said, "How do I look? All right? Or is something wrong with this dress?"

Mrs. Tabb gave it her grave consideration. "I see nothing wrong with it, Miss Lisa. It suits you, I will say that!"

Lisa was so frustrated. "Dr. Lee would snort at it, if he bothered to look at me at all!" she burst out.

"Oh, don't take any notice of your father-in-law, my dear. Liver's a right nasty thing to have."

"What else *could* I wear for the mornings?" Lisa fretted.

"What did you wear in London, before you met Mr. Andrew?" Mrs. Tabb asked, in her best practical tone.

"Twin sets and suits. On warm days I used to sunbathe in the garden or the local lido," Lisa offered.

"I shouldn't try to do that here," Mrs. Tabb said severely. "I shouldn't worry about how you look, anyway. What does it matter?"

Mrs. Tabb hadn't noticed what she had said, that was very evident. She hummed a tuneless air under her breath as she finished clearing, and she waddled out without another glance in Lisa's direction.

But Lisa remembered it and pondered over it. Why should anyone say it didn't matter how she looked? Was there a reason, or was it just that Mrs. Tabb didn't want to be bothered with what seemed a frivolous problem?

Lisa remembered it especially as the week slid by and Andrew didn't settle on that promised day off. And when it came to the point, he said, in a bothered sort of voice, "Does it have to be this week, my dear? I know I ought to take a regular day off, but if you weren't here, I wouldn't, because it means my father has to take over in case of emergency."

"What's wrong with the other doctors in the town?" she asked fiercely. "In London they used to help each other out, or else the patients had to go to hospital in emergency while the doctor was having a few hours off."

"That was London. Bigger service, different arrangements," he said, but Lisa couldn't help feeling that he was deliberately going without his day off because he had thought better of his rash promise to tell her all the things she wanted to know.

"All right, you work, Andrew. You work yourself silly and don't be surprised if you get laid up yourself. It isn't sense to drive yourself like this!"

"Well, if it's all that important to you, Lisa, I suppose I'd better take a bit of time off but I really can't manage a whole day."

"Then don't you bother, Andrew. Not for me! I don't count!"

"What do you mean – you don't count? Aren't you well, Lisa? Or are you trying to quarrel with me? You can't be so disappointed!"

"No, I'm not disappointed," she said, her chin in the air. "I can find plenty to do. I'll go to the farm and see Carmichael – he said I could any time."

She wasn't looking at Andrew, and so she didn't notice the odd startled look that leapt into his eyes.

She rushed on, now she had started, unable to stop: "Or I can go to the hospital and see the organist – they seem to think he'd be pleased to see me, though I can't think why. And there's Zillie Denner wanting me to play his piano for him, and I've got a standing invitation at the vicarage mending the hymn books. Life is so madly exciting around here!" and she slammed out of the room.

She hadn't meant to do that. But now she had. Now she had quarrelled with her beloved Andrew.

With tears stinging her eyes, she picked up her purse and her jacket and ran out of the house, through the square and into the High Street.

At the bus stop people were waiting. She joined the queue. She must go somewhere, be on the move, do something, to take her mind off the situation at The Old House.

When the bus came, it was marked 'Alicia Mawson Memorial Hospital.' Interest sparked in Lisa as she recalled that the Mawson family had once been rich local people and had been responsible for the park. So they had had a finger in the hospital, too, had they? She decided to go and have a look at the place.

That was when she recalled that the organist must be in there, and that she had not yet honoured her promise to the vicar to go and see him. Well, it was mid-week; the people climbing with her on to the bus were all talking about things which suggested that they, too, were visitors to the hospital. Lisa joined them, and listened to them, feeling less apart and lonely than she usually did.

The hospital was a mixture of old and new. It took an hour for the bus to get there, yet it couldn't have been more than twenty five minutes journey in a car. The bus wound round in circles doubling back on secondary roads, stopping to pick up shoppers-on-wheels and push-chairs; even waiting at one corner for a rheumaticky old fellow to stump down the path from his house, because this was his regular trip.

Lisa sauntered in with the rest of the people, and followed suit, stopping at a stall of flowers and fruit, to buy. She couldn't go in without taking something, yet she had no idea what sort of person he was, or what he would be like. She should have told Hazel she was coming, got briefed, and taken a message.

She asked for Nigel Franklin, and she was directed to his ward at once. Everyone, it seemed, knew the organist of St. Anne's in Queensmarket.

He was in the corner bed; one leg and one arm were suspended, and there was a cage over his other leg.

"Mrs. Lee?" he began, with a nice smile. He was a man of some thirty-five years, but his plain, rather long face looked younger, boyish, a trusting face. He held out his undamaged arm to shake hands with her. "It was very good of you to come. The vicar said in one of his letters that you'd promised to."

Lisa warmed to him. Unlike everyone else, he treated her as an ordinary kindly soul who had offered to visit him; he didn't seem to realise that she was anyone unusual, such as the successor to that first wife of Andrew's.

Lisa shook hands with him and said, "What happened to you? Are you sure you feel well enough to chatter?"

"Oh, good heavens, yes. I've been looking forward to it, actually," he admitted. "You're a friend of Hazel's aren't you? Didn't she tell you what happened to me?"

Lisa shook her head.

"She spends most of her time warding off my questions because, d'you see, I'm a stranger to the district."

"Oh, then you won't know – keep clear of the lighthouse. I fell down the steps."

"You *what*?"

"Yes, well, I was looking for the lighthouse keeper – he has rather a fine voice and I wanted him for the choir. He hasn't much to do when he comes off duty. But I couldn't find him."

"Go on," Lisa urged.

He looked confused. "Oh, well, it's a long story. Are you sure Hazel didn't tell you about it?"

"No, she didn't tell me a thing about it. I didn't know even why you were in here. I know she wants you to come back."

That wasn't the right thing to say, though she hadn't meant to couch it in the wrong way. His face lit up at once. "She does? Are you sure — or are you just saying so?"

"We all want you back," Lisa hastily amended. "Me specially — I'm playing the organ, and I'm not much good at it. And Hazel can't control the choir-boys and the vicar can't concentrate on his Chess with Dr. Lee, and Dr. Lee hates his game to be messed up and takes it out of the rest of us, and there you are. It's a vicious circle."

He had to laugh, in spite of his disappointment. "I say, you're rather jolly, aren't you? I'm so glad, because I couldn't stand Dr.Andrew's first wife."

And he blushed right up to the roots of his hair.

Lisa's eyes lit up. "You've actually mentioned her. You're positively the first one who has said a thing about her, without me having to drag it out of them. Oh, do please tell me all about her. What she looked like, what she used to talk about, everything about her."

"I've opened my big mouth again," he said unhappily. "Oh, dear, just when I thought I'd conquered the habit. Hazel hasn't any patience with me, you know. She's pretty blunt herself but never tactless. I say, don't tell her, or she'll roast me next time she comes. *If* she comes again, which I doubt, because she went for me last time about the same thing."

"Oh, but she can't – not while you're in hospital like this," Lisa protested.

"She says that what happened to me was my own fault but," he said, with a huge grin, "I say it was hers. I told her so, and she didn't like that. Oh, well, now what am I going to do? Will you forgive me and try to forget about it?"

"Yes, if you tell me a few things about the first Mrs. Lee. How long have you been organist, to remember her?"

"Years and years," he said affably. "I've always lived here, you see. Started as the smallest (and most awful little wretch) in the choir, and worked my way up, till I went away to study music. Then I gravitated back. Had my chance to go to other places, but somehow when you once get bitten by the Queensmarket bug, you can't get away. It's quite a lovely old town, you know."

"Perhaps I'm prejudiced. I'm homesick for London, and I haven't had much of a welcome since I came here."

"Oh, I say! Hasn't Hazel – ?"

"Yes! Hazel is one of the few people who really has made me feel I was wanted," Lisa told him.

"And you like music, so you must have met Zillie Denner. He's a jolly nice old boy, don't you think?"

"Yes, I do. He's a friend of mine already. He lets me play his grand piano, and we have cocoa together. I like Martin Biddell, too, and of course, Carmichael Mawson – I only met him once, but he was very nice. But you see, even those few people are rather odd in their manner, when it comes to the point of who I am, or if something is mentioned that I guess concerns Andrew's first wife."

"Well, yes, they would be, wouldn't they, especially Carmichael Mawson," he mused.

"But why, *why*?"

"I wish you'd ask Hazel. I shall only go and say something we'll be sorry for."

"Hazel says she didn't know Tressida."

"You know her name?" He was plainly astonished.

"Carmichael Mawson let it out. He didn't mean to, and he was cross that he did."

"I bet he was," Nigel Franklin said feelingly. "No, no, don't ask me why, or I shall run on, and get myself into deep water."

"Well, tell me what she was *like*. It's my guess that she was the exact opposite to me, in colouring and everything, except that she must have liked music."

"*Liked it*?" He pulled a face. "Oh, I wouldn't say that. Look, why are you so concerned about her? Is it something that's happened that I don't know about?"

Lisa was about to tell him how old Dr. Lee seemed to dislike her, but Nigel broke in as an afterthought, "No, don't tell me. It's sure to be personal and I shall go and blab it to someone and then you'll be fed up with me and you won't come again, and I would like you to. Oh, damn, there goes the bell for All Out."

"Please tell me, before I go – what was she like?" Lisa pleaded.

"Well, she was very beautiful," Nigel burst out, as if it was prompted by someone else and not him at all. "And I absolutely refuse to say any more. I say, do try and persuade Hazel to come with you next time."

"Shall I ask her to come alone?" Lisa suggested.

"I didn't mean that. I'd like to see you, too, but if there are the two of you, I shan't argue with her and I shan't say all the wrong things to you."

She left him, laughing at him. She had liked him, but it was so aggravating to think that he had known Tressida Lee so well and couldn't tell Lisa a thing about her.

She stood outside looking at a big stone statue of one of the Mawsons, and one of the other visitors stopped to look at it, too. A young woman with a country accent. Someone who didn't stare at her as if mentally comparing her with that other girl called Lee.

"Did the Mawsons really build this hospital?" Lisa was moved to ask her. "Or don't you know?"

"Oh, yes, I know," the other said slowly, a smile dawning. "My old grandfather used to say that if it wasn't for the Mawsons, we'd have fared badly for hospitals, on account of no other hospital in miles, in them days. Of course, it was the first hospital – not this one – that the Mawsons founded – quite a small one – and you'll not see much of it now. Just the front bit of the building. The big hospital that's built on behind was done later, and not by the Mawsons. That was after they lost most of their money and the family broke up."

"How did they lose their money? And when?" Lisa asked, thinking of that nice Carmichael, and the way he had spoken of the Lees, and of Tressida.

"Well, it was a tragic family. Seemly you're a stranger in these parts, not to know about them. But there, she was the only girl, and the boys would naturally put all they had in, to hush up a scandal like that. I feel right sorry for them, though. Broke the old man's heart, and when he died, the mother wasn't long after him. Only one stayed behind to tend the farm. He wouldn't give up the land, not that had been Mawson land for so long. Oh, there goes my bus – I'll cut through the alley and catch it coming round into the square. Goodbye, then."

There it was again – leaving her just when it was getting interesting, Lisa fumed. So the Mawsons had had their troubles, too. Did Andrew know about that? He must know about them – he had kept in touch with his father, hadn't he? Then why wasn't he being friends with Carmichael? Why didn't Carmichael come to The Old House, as he had used to do? It was all very puzzling and unsatisfactory.

Lisa caught her bus back to Queensmarket in a very different frame of mind than when she had gone. All the anger had evaporated. She had met another pleasant person – the organist of St. Anne's – and she had got a lot to tell Hazel the next time she went to he vicarage.

It was too late for tea at The Old House

when the bus pulled up in Queensmarket High Street, and too early for the evening meal. Lisa felt a little flutter of anger that she, a young married woman, couldn't go back to her own home and make a cup of tea and cut a cheese sandwich to tide her over to the evening meal. But of course, it wasn't her own home. It was the home of her father-in-law, and his housekeeper was so set in her ways that if Lisa asked for one crumb between meals there would be a large-scale storm.

She decided to go to a café she had seen, which boasted a sign 'Open until midnight'. It was a little like being in London, at one of the old milk bars. Lisa nostalgically ordered a bowl of celery soup, a crusty roll and butter, a wedge of cheese, and a hunk of iced chocolate cake to eat instead of pudding. The coffee smelt good, too, and while she made inroads into the soup, she stared out at the home-going people in the High Street.

In the next three days she had to visit the houses of her piano pupils. Two she hadn't even met. Tonight she was to renew her struggle with the Pendleton child, and that meant a bus both ways. It was too much to hope she might run into Carmichael Mawson again.

A young woman came in and perched on the stool beside her; a young woman with a good-looking, clean-cut but very decisive face, and a lean, strong young body in fine sweater and jodhpurs, and when she spoke to the man dressed as a chef behind the counter, her voice was a clean-cut and decisive as the rest of her.

"Some soup, Bert, and see it's hot, will you?"

"Why, Miss Gregory, what are you doing in here at this time? Didn't you get any mid-day meal?" he asked her.

"No. Don't talk to me about food! I've been up at Maceys all the morning with that confounded cow, and I've just realised I've had nothing to eat. Piles of corned beef sandwiches, Bert, thick as you like, to follow the soup."

And then she said something that made Lisa turn round sharply and look straight at her. "Have you seen Andrew Lee today, Bert? He's the most elusive person, and I haven't got time to – "

Bert shook his head fiercely and slid

an eye round to Lisa. "He's not been in to see the missus today Miss Gregory, her being better, but this here happens to be the new Mrs. Lee. Right, am I?" he smiled at Lisa. "Thought so."

"How did you know who I was?" Lisa asked. This man was the last person she would have thought would know her. He was well down the High Street, among the multiple stores and the crowds of people who came in from the other towns.

The man grinned. Not a face she could like or trust, but he seemed pleasant enough. "Well, I get the wife's medicine made up at Biddell's, see, and you were coming out as I came in, and I heard the chemist say to his assistant who you were."

Lisa felt a prick of uneasiness. What else had Martin said to his assistant, to make this man so sure that it was the doctor's new wife?

The vet. didn't give her time for much reflection. Whatever she had been about to say about Andrew, she recovered herself quickly, and held out her hand to Lisa, taking it in a grasp that almost broke Lisa's small bones.

"Heavens, it took us long enough to meet, didn't it?" she said, with a short bark of a laugh. "Lisa, isn't it? I'm Dinah. I suppose Andrew's mentioned me often enough?"

Had he? Lisa couldn't remember him doing so. And if this girl thought he should have, why? What was the connection?

"Possibly, but there have been so many new names to learn, and in such a short while," Lisa said. "I'm very glad to meet you now, though, even if it's a little odd, this place, for a first meeting. Shall we be seeing you at The Old House?"

The girl's lips twitched, and the man behind the counter made a slight choking noise, as if smothering a laugh. He took himself off to serve another customer, and he put on the radio, a shade too loud, as if to give Dinah Gregory more privacy for what she had to say to Lisa. More than ever Lisa felt she didn't like this man, which was a pity, for she had been enjoying her meal.

Dinah kept on eating hers, while she talked. "I don't think you will, somehow.

It's a little matter of your father-in-law. He hates me."

"Then we have something in common," Lisa said. "He isn't terribly taken with me, either."

Dinah looked surprised at that, and considered Lisa. "Well, no, I suppose he wouldn't be, come to think of it," she said, after a half insolent gaze of appraisal. "I wonder why Andrew married you? On the rebound, I suppose. Oh, don't mind me being blunt, my dear. I'm famous for it, in these parts. At least you know where you stand with me."

Hazel Edwards had said much the same thing about her own bluntness, but she hadn't been insulting like this girl, Lisa recalled.

"Of course, Andrew was so much in love with his first wife that no-one could expect him to be in love again, but who cares about rebounds? It's as good a way to catch a husband as any, and time makes people get used to each other."

Lisa slid down from the stool. She had lost her appetite. "I'm sure you must be right," she said coldly. "Goodbye — I have to be getting back."

She hurried out of the milk-bar, but Dinah's mocking voice came after her. "What for? Andrew isn't there, and Mrs. Tabb won't want to see you too soon."

How true, but Dinah Gregory had no need to say it, or to call it out so that everyone in the café heard it.

She had no key to The Old House, and Mrs. Tabb hated to be brought through from the kitchen quarters unless it was urgent. So Lisa wandered round the house, and found a slightly open window and got in. How like everything in this place – nothing arranged for her, the new wife, not even a spare key!

She went quietly up to her room, changed and went out. They could keep their beastly evening meal. Anyway, she didn't want to see another bite of food this side of bedtime. That Dinah Gregory had taken her appetite away.

She caught a bus to the Pendleton house, and by the time she had walked the last stretch of the way from the bus stop to the house, it was time for the lesson to begin.

There was the usual unrewarding

struggle with Patricia and the usual half-hearted offer for the child's father to drive Lisa home. She firmly refused, and kept walking until the next bus came along.

It was late when she arrived back at the house. She found that Dr. Lee had retired early to his room, and Andrew was looking at the last copy but one of *The Lancet.* A tray of sandwiches was by his side, and a flask of coffee.

At the sound of her coming into the room, he jumped up and threw the magazine away.

"Where have you been, Lisa?" he demanded angrily. "There's been an awful row because you didn't let Mrs. Tabb know you wouldn't be in to dinner. You might have a little more consideration."

She considered this, and said, "I went to the hospital to see the organist."

"What on earth for?" he was surprised, not at all pleased, and there was a dawning look in his eyes that Lisa couldn't pin down. Almost as if he hadn't expected Lisa, of all people, to do the thing which had displeased him.

"I told you before – because the vicar

asked me to," she said collectedly. "He reminded me that he was a close friend of your father's and he more or less expected me to agree to go, though I didn't much want to."

"Oh," Andrew subsided, then flared up again because of the lateness of the hour. "Where have you been since?"

"Giving the Pendleton child a piano lesson, to please Hazel Edwards," Lisa said. Now she was getting angry. "I had to catch a bus to get there, and wait for a bus back. It's an hourly service."

"Why didn't you take a cab?" he asked, blankly.

"I hadn't enough money for a cab. I'd spent the rest of the money I had from my last music lesson."

"Why didn't you say so? Have I ever refused to give money?"

At any other time Lisa would have realised how tired and anxious he was, to carry on like this, but at this moment, after her own none too happy day, she only saw the injustice of his question.

"How could you, since I've never asked you for any?" she flared. "In London you paid the bills by cash, and I drew on my music pupils fees for my own ready cash. Since I've been here, it's been quite a clever feat to get you alone long enough to say hallo, let alone to make arrangements about money!"

At that moment, Mrs. Tabb came in, with the sketchiest of knocks on the door and without waiting to be requested to enter or refused. She folded her hands in front of her and looked accusingly at Lisa. She had come in, hearing Lisa's voice, to have her own say about Lisa's absence from the evening meal.

Andrew turned round on the housekeeper. "Not now, Mrs. Tabb. Take it up with Lisa in the morning. I am discussing something with her at the moment, or trying to!"

Mrs. Tabb looked offended and went out.

"There you are, you see!" Lisa flared. "You refer to me as Lisa, to *her*! And she speaks to me as if I were a schoolgirl. I'll never have any standing in this place at all if you go on like that. Don't you tell me to shut up, Andrew! People in the street talk to me as if I'm someone here on sufferance! Do you know that someone told me today that I only caught you on the rebound, because you loved your first wife so much that you'd never love anyone else? How about that?"

She was almost beside herself now with rage and misery, and his attitude didn't help.

She didn't know that he had already had words with his father and with Mrs. Tabb, defending Lisa, and he was worn out with the pressure of work on him since he had come here.

"Who would say such a thing to you, Lisa?"

"Dinah Gregory. The vet," she said, watching him.

His anger slid away. "Dinah? Said that? Oh, come Lisa, you must have misunderstood what she said. Dinah would never say such a thing."

"But she did! In the hearing of the man behind the counter in the milk bar. He knew me but I didn't know him."

He stared hard at her, and came over to her, to put his hand on her forehead. "You can't be well," he said.

She pushed his hand away. "I didn't think you'd take it like that. You like that girl, don't you?"

"Dinah? Yes, she's all right. We grew up together. Now just you calm down, Lisa, and try and think what it was she did say. Not that, or anything like it, I'm pretty sure."

"Yes she did, and I'm beginning to believe it's true. Don't look so shocked. Just think of my position for a moment. I came here without a murmur, because you wanted to. Uprooted myself from my home, my friends, my music pupils. All I had, just to come with you. And what's it been like since I've been here? It's not my house – I'm not even allowed to do the washing-up. I haven't any money, any position, any standing in the eyes of the local people. Bless me, I haven't even a husband, not in the proper sense. That was all arranged for me by the housekeeper! I must be all sorts of a fool to put up with it. But I'm not going to, not any more."

"Lisa, Lisa, will you shut up? You're overwrought," he said, taking her by the shoulders and shaking her. "I think you'd better sleep by yourself for just one more night, after all, which is a pity, because I've been chasing Mrs. Tabb to get that other room ready, if only temporarily, and somehow, heaven help me, I managed to push her into doing just that."

10

MRS. TABB came in to see why Lisa was crying, but again Andrew dismissed her. "If you want to help, perhaps you'd bring some hot milk and a biscuit," he said shortly.

Mrs. Tabb, deeply resentful that her beloved Andrew was ordering her about like this, promptly blamed it on to Lisa. She brought back the milk with ill grace, and wasn't pleased when Andrew asked for hot water bottles to be put in Lisa's bed.

"Please Andrew," Lisa whispered, as Mrs. Tabb again went out, "please – there's only one thing that will be any use to me tonight. To be allowed to be with you. You said you'd made her get the other room ready. Please let's, Andrew, please let's."

He hesitated before her passionate pleading, and finally gave in. "Very well, then, but if you show any signs of being upset, my dear, I shall leave you and go into the dressing-room. We neither of us can afford to lose a night's sleep over useless questions and recriminations. What's done is done."

"Yes Andrew," she whispered, and obediently sipped her milk.

The big room which Mrs. Tabb had been persuaded to get ready, was indeed badly in need of redecoration, but as Andrew muttered under his breath, it was a mystery to him why the builders hadn't managed to come in before now and do the wall papering and the ceiling. It wasn't such a big job, after all.

Lisa looked at the faded wallpaper with its sprawling roses and Victorian ribbon bows trailing among them. Mauve and grey and what had once been silver, and a very faded grey paint. Not inspiring, but she was with Andrew again, and she for one wasn't going to complain. She got undressed, and as a gesture, she put on her brand-new cream nylon nightie with the lace frills threaded with narrow black ribbon, and tied her long brown hair up in a cream chiffon scarf. She looked at herself in the mirror in a bothered way. She ought to be putting on night cream, she supposed, or taking off false eye lashes. She conceded to this new mood by putting on a dab of perfume, but it was so unfamiliar that she wished she hadn't. Scented soap for her bath was as far as she usually went. Andrew would think she had gone mad.

She got into bed and waited for him. He came in from his old dressing-room in a new silk dressing-gown, a paisley scarf tucked in at the neck. As always she was aware of how tall he was, and how distinguished he looked. Why, why had he married her?

He stood there, looking down at her, with such an odd expression on his face. Then he sat on the side of the bed beside her.

"I'm sorry I shouted at you, Lisa," he began, taking one of her hands in the old way and fondling it.

She was so overcome, that she could only say in a choked voice, "That's all right. I shouted at you."

"I was worried about you. This is a strange town to you. Heaven knew what you had done with yourself. Mrs. Tabb said I wasn't to worry. She had some garbled story of your coming in through a window. I got very angry with her over that. It hasn't been very comfortable here today." He sighed. "I'd give the world to make you happy, and when you come home and say things to me about my not loving you, as you did tonight, I feel I've failed horribly."

Tears rained down her cheeks again. It was no use insisting that Dinah Gregory had said just that. It was no use admitting that she had climbed in a window, because it would raise the issue of a key, and her position in the house, and one thing would lead to another, and it would spoil this promising beginning. So she just sat there in bed, staring dumbly at him, wishing with all her heart that they could be transported back to No. 19, and hear the familiar sounds of that cosy little street, such as the revving up of Johnny Miles' motorbike and the muted wail of his brother Roddy's trumpet as he practised for his beat group. Here there was the howling of the wind coming in from the North Sea, and the low moan of the receding tide and a solitary fog horn somewhere, a long way away.

Perhaps Andrew appreciated this dimly.

"You're not happy here, are you, Lisa?"

"I would be, if I had you," she whispered.

"Well, you have got me, silly sweet," he said, and drew her into his arms, and kissed her; soft butterfly kisses starting on the tip of her nose and touching her closed eyelids her forehead, her chin. He began to whisper the silly little things he used to, in those first blissful months of their marriage.

She was still too tense, and he knew it. He raised his head and looked at her, and she caught her breath. What was he going to do? Ask questions, which would lead to a quarrel? Or was he going to decide that she ought to sleep alone?

She ought to ask him questions, now she had him alone. There were so many things she wanted to know, had the right to know. But instinct prompted her to keep silent. So far, so good. She had no idea what had been going on today, to prompt him to push Mrs. Tabb into doing what she hadn't wanted to about the room, but Lisa felt that if she said just one word more, it would throw out the delicate balance of Andrew's change of mood, and she might never progress as far as this again.

So she just sat miserably staring at him, unaware that her eyes spoke such volumes that all the resolutions he had made about their marriage now that they were back in this district, flew out of his head, and he knew that there was only one thing he wanted in all the world. That was Lisa, and the comfortable new existence she had given him back in that small suburban street in London.

He stood up and began to deliberately peel off his dressing-gown and the scarf, and then he put out the light.

Lisa didn't sleep much that night. Andrew lay half sprawled across her, and his deep regular breathing close to her ear temporarily blotted out the more distant sounds of sea and fog-horn. These sounds were blanketed by a white mist that had crept in from the sea. There was a faint smell of seaweed and fog finding its way in through the chink where the window didn't quite shut, but it was warm in bed, and for the first time for weeks, she felt really secure.

It was true that she hadn't seized the

opportunity to ask him all the things she had wanted to know about his past, but that would have been lunacy. It was enough to feel the touch of his hands, his mouth, and to hear his voice, thick with tenderness and desire, as it had been once. What did it matter if that ghost haunted her in the day-time, if sometimes she could have Andrew, like this, at night? At last she fell asleep and for once she didn't dream.

She awoke late. When she went downstairs for breakfast, he was already in surgery. Mrs. Tabb, stiff with disapproval was waiting to serve Lisa's breakfast.

She was hungry, but it wouldn't be wise to ask for anything hot now, so she said hastily. "I'll just have a glass of milk and some fruit, Mrs. Tabb. Honestly — that's all I want."

Mrs. Tabb served her without argument. It was plain that Lisa was not really her concern. It was only Andrew who needed porridge and a good hot breakfast every morning, winter or summer alike, in her opinion.

Still, in spite of that unpromising start, Lisa was happy. So happy that she braved the rather chilly day with its damp salt-laden wind and penetrating sea-spray to walk along the shore beyond the park, and to look in on everyone she already knew, except of course Carmichael who would be working and not likely to welcome callers in the morning.

Martin Biddell was pleased to see her, but he was snowed under with prescriptions from Andrew and the other doctors in the town, so she didn't wait. Zillie, however, wasn't busy, so she stayed for cocoa with him.

"You look very lovely this morning," he announced. "And you blush like the women of my country. I think that you are perhaps giving it time, and as I have told you many times, time is a great healer."

"I dare say you're right," she told him. "But I would like to go back to London. I don't suppose it would matter if I just popped up there for a day, to see how things were getting on," she said, half to herself. "It's funny, come to think of it, that we haven't heard."

She told him about Mrs. Cobb, who was looking after the house until she heard about her passage to Australia to her son. “I suppose I’ve rather left it to Andrew, and I expect he’s been so busy. If he thought about it at all, I suppose he’d be inclined to leave it to me, as it’s my house.”

Zillie had a happy thought. “Ask your good husband to take you to London on his next day off.”

“I might, if he took a day off,” she retorted.

“But he – ” Zillie began, looking surprised, then he quickly turned it aside. “But he is working too hard, he should take a day off” he amended it. “You must make him. You are his wife.”

“I think it’s a very good idea, Zillie. I’ll do what I can. Yes, that would be lovely. We might stay there the night and do a show. I don’t see why his father shouldn’t take morning surgery for once.” She glanced at Zillie. “It’s wonderful the way he’s perked up since we came here, taking all those long walks. In fact, if I weren’t generous I might not think there was much the matter with him.”

Zillie knew how to be careful when it came to commenting on Dr. Lee’s health.

"If he seems better, then it is a thing to thank heaven for, no?"

Today she played him some Chopin. He was quick to notice the choice. It matched her mood. A strange, exciting mood that was half happiness, half sadness. She had had Andrew last night, close and secure for such a little while. If she had thought about the next day at all, she would have been sure he would kiss her, refer to those hours of darkness and pleasure. But to just leave her, go to the surgery without a word, had staggered and scared her. Just how near had she got to him last night after all?

Still, the mood of elation wouldn't entirely leave her, and it rushed over her anew as, after leaving Zillie's antique shop, she went through the passage to the churchyard, and decided to look Hazel up.

Hazel noticed the change in her at once. "Hello, what's up? You look as if you'd lost a tanner and found half a crown."

"The vicar's daughter," Lisa scolded, clucking in disapproval. "You really should be a little more elegant, Hazel."

They sat down laughing together, and inevitably Hazel made tea and brought out the fruit cake that had been made only yesterday. "Have you come to try and get out of organ practice or something?"

"No, of course not. Besides, it's my new pupils today, remember?" Lisa protested with her mouth full.

"Oh, yes, those Kidman kids. Was I responsible for that? I forget."

"Was it you? Or was it Amy Clickett? Anyway, what's wrong with them?"

"What's right," Hazel retorted. "They're twins. Boy and a girl. Eleven. Real shockers. Audrey and Bernie. Watch your step with them. You need not take them on if you don't want to, but you know what a small place like this is like. If you're choosey it gets around. I rather thought you wanted to be occupied at any price."

"I do. Where do they live, and how do I get there?"

"You'll have to go by car unless you want to hang about for an hour and a half. It's a rotten bus service at that time of night. It's on the way to the hospital. I suppose I ought to go and see Nigel."

"That reminds me – I went, yesterday afternoon," and she told Hazel some of what happened.

Hazel looked very bothered. "I say, that was good of you."

"He's very nice. But why the secret about what happened to him? He says I am to ask you about it."

"Did he! He thinks he's in love with me. It clouds his judgment so don't take too much notice of what he says."

"Only *thinks* he's in love with you? Sure you aren't a little bit in love with him?"

"Nope. I have my head screwed on the right way. It comes of being a vicar's daughter and seeing how people live on a shoe-string. Not for me. And being the organist's wife won't be much different. Beside, we'd fight. Does that strike you as the right thing?"

"They say true love never runs smooth. I would have dismissed that as the corniest remark ever made, until recently," Lisa said slowly. "I don't know. I suppose you know best, but I'm glad you're going tonight. Yes, you are – you just said you supposed you'd have to go."

"That doesn't mean I've made up my mind to," Hazel said flushing.

"How would it be if you did go, just the same, and dropped me at this Kidman house on the way? You can pick me up coming back."

"That ties me up for visiting very nicely, doesn't it?" Hazel said bitterly. "You matchmaker, you. You'll be sorry."

"Maybe I will. All matchmakers deserve to be. Anyway there's another thing I want to ask you. Can you recommend a good hairdresser – one who can lift my face at the same time, or make it over or something."

"What's the matter with you today?" Hazel gasped, pausing in the act of taking a second hunk of cake to her mouth.

"My dear father-in-law said to me a few days ago something about why didn't I go to a hairdressers or do whatever a woman does to make herself look older. He seems to think look too young to be a doctor's wife. I think he also meant I was too plain to replace the other one."

Hazel looked really distressed. "Oh, Lisa, why don't you stop talking to people about her? Who told you she wasn't plain?"

Lisa didn't say. She didn't want to get the organist into worse trouble with Hazel. But Hazel guessed.

"It was that Nigel. I know it. I can read it in your face. Oh, that fellow. Do you know he thinks he's going to be a successful newspaper man. There never was a bigger mistake he could make. You can't be a newspaper man when you don't know how to keep your mouth shut."

Lisa looked surprised. "Is he on a newspaper? He didn't say."

"Well, there wouldn't be enough for him to do, just being organist to this small parish. He has got one or two pupils learning the organ, but writing for the press has always been a dream of his. Oh, that man. Lisa, do think twice and don't have anything done to that nice hair and face of yours," she begged.

"Tell me the hairdresser's name. I shall need one, won't I?"

"What for? Wash your hair yourself, and leave it nice and straight. It suits you."

"I shall need it trimmed," Lisa insisted.

Hazel sighed. "I go to Maison Robert in the High Street, but you'd better go to Pierre Perronier in Monks Rawley if you want a good cut. They can't trim for toffee in the High Street."

She scrabbled in a drawer for the telephone number but Lisa stopped her. "Don't bother. I've nothing to do for the rest of the day so I might as well go to Monks Rawley. Andrew says I'm to get about and see the district. Oh, I forgot – he didn't give me any money. That settles it then. I'm broke."

Hazel said, "No you're not. I don't know what you'd do without me to look after you, though. Here you are," and she counted out some silver into Lisa's outstretched hand. "Money for two lessons from the Pendletons."

"I don't understand. I usually send a bill in at the end of the term," Lisa protested.

"Not here, if you've got any sense. Hold your hand out for cash at the end of each lesson. Especially in that house. Otherwise you'll never get it. Don't be misled by the air of affluence. They don't like paying up, full stop."

"Then how did you come by this?" Lisa asked.

"I had to go over there to collect stuff for the next Jumble Sale and I asked them for your money, during the course of conversation," she finished, pulling a face.

"And do you mean to tell me I have to ask for my money tonight at the Kidmans?"

"They will expect it," Hazel said firmly.

It was nice to have some spare cash again, though it wouldn't go far, but as it happened, Andrew remembered at lunch time. He gave Lisa five pounds. "Don't go out without money on you again," he said severely, and pulled her into his arms to kiss her. But the telephone rang and with a muttered remark under his breath which she couldn't catch, he went to answer it.

"That means," he said, coming away from the instrument, "that I shall be out most of the rest of today. The Brickett's fourth's on the way."

"Four babies. How lovely," Lisa breathed, and couldn't quite meet his eyes.

"You wouldn't want brats around you,

Lisa," he said at last. "You're only a child yourself," and he had gone before she could think of a suitable reply.

She remembered then that she hadn't told him where she would be for the rest of the day, so she wrote a note and put it on his desk in the surgery. "Monks Rawley this afternoon, Kidman's twins this evening, Hazel driving me there and back." Because it wasn't very private in the surgery, she refrained from peppering the note with little crosses to denote kisses, as she had been used to do at No. 19. There she had pinned them to the curtains, the cushions of his favourite armchair, or tucked in the brim of his favourite off-duty hat, a rakish pork pie, hairy, a grey-ish green. She remembered that hat with nostalgia, but he had, for some reason, left it behind when they had come here.

As an afterthought, she came back and wrote, 'P.S. Have you done anything about Mrs. Cobb at No. 19 — I forgot."

That afternoon the sun shone. The sea glittered. Part of the bus route ran near the coast and they crawled for a long time in the narrow road behind a wide farm waggon, until it turned down a lane.

Monks Rawley was very old, and most of the buildings were of grey stone. Not a very promising town, Lisa thought for a smart hairdresser's, and when she came to it, she didn't like the look of it. She wondered why Hazel had recommended it and could only think it was to discourage her from wanting to do anything about her hair.

Lisa wandered through the town, watching a motorist go down a one-way street and have to back out again because a lorry had got stuck in the other end, and she idled away some time watching the solitary traffic policeman trying to clear a jam in the narrow main street because of parked vehicles outside of shops. Not a town she would care to drive though, she thought.

At last, bored and tired of walking around, she got on another bus and tried Skegwell.

Skegwell was a rip-roaring town for trippers. It had everything, including a stone-walled harbour, a squatty lighthouse on the end of it, a boating pool for the children, a fine shopping centre and a baleful wind off the North Sea that roared along the stone promenade and made the flowers in the laid-out beds hunch together as if they were trying to turn their heads down into the earth again and hide.

Lisa hunched her shoulders against the wind and left the shore, to explore the shops. And here she found the hairdressers she had been searching for.

It was a very large establishment and she found there was a free assistant who was prepared to do things to her hair and face without argument.

She sat there with her eyes closed while they snipped and clipped – an enthusiastic young man, and a girl who joined him to give her the manicure she suddenly decided she must have.

"A golden rinse would be right for madame," the young man said.

"The Chinese look for madame's eyes," the girl pronounced.

Someone (Lisa wasn't sure which of them) suggested she should have a regular appointment and to open an account with them. Lisa had been wondering whether she would have enough money for all this and was glad of the suggestion. But in making out the details of the account, when the name and address were mentioned, the atmosphere changed. Subtly, without any distress; just a quickening of interest.

"Mrs. Lee? Oh, we used to have another young Mrs. Lee. Some years ago. That would be — yes, that would be in Francie's time. Francie did her hair regularly. Oh, she was very beautiful. A relative, perhaps? Tragic end, though. Tragic. But that colour hair, and those eyes — "

Lisa sat very still. So this was why Hazel had tried to dissuade her, and had finally mentioned that place in Monks Rawley. *This* was the establishment that Tressida had come to. But of course, she would.

She was dying to ask *what* colour hair, *what* colour eyes, but she didn't. She made sympathetic noises, said she believed it was someone in the family, and prompted the garrulous young man to go on talking.

"You must go to Reginald Dyers — *she* got her clothes from there. Very smart establishment, Reginald Dyers."

"And she always went into the Honey Bar afterwards, to meet a friend, for an aperitif. Has madame tried the Honey Bar?"

Some devil in Lisa drove her to go to all the places afterwards that Tressida had frequented. In all of them was a preponderance of mirrors, and the new Lisa stared back with wilful and improbable promise. She didn't like what she had allowed them to do to her but it was too late now. They had cut her hair so that it swirled upwards to one side and curved capriciously over one eye. Her eyes were shadowed so that instead of looking wide and innocent any more, they were sultry, inviting. How, Lisa asked herself could that mask of a face portray feelings that weren't there?

At the emporium the buyer remembered Tressida, looked Lisa over critically and brought out a dress that Lisa would never have dreamed of buying, with the remark, "Oh, yes, *this* is for madame," Still, the over-modern dress was better suited to what had been done to her in the hairdresser's.

Her own simple shirt-waister had been a mockery of innocence, foiling as it did the sophistication of her head and face.

With a new purse and high sling-back sandals, she walked down the great street of shops to the hotel on the corner, where the Honey Bar was advertised in neon lighting.

She went inside and climbed on to a high stool and drank a tomato juice. If Dr. Lee's first wife had come here and done this, then surely it was all right for Dr. Lee's second wife?

She longed above all for a cup of tea. Sweet and strong, with buttered crumpets. The little cosy meal she and Andrew had enjoyed so much during the week-ends in those early days of their marriage. Not such a long time ago, in all conscience, but already it was seeming like years.

As she sat dreaming, a man strolled in and sat on the stool beside her. His insolent smile raked her from top to toe, and told her without need for words that he liked what he saw.

He had a rather battered face, and his eyes were hooded, yet he couldn't have been much older than Andrew. His features were too blurred, and his eyes were a faded blue. Something faintly familiar about him made her look intently up into his face, which he promptly misconstrued.

"I know a better place than this," he murmured, "unless you know someone better to kill time with."

Lisa whipped herself out of her bemused frame of mind and scrambled down from her stool. "Actually I'm meeting someone," she said, and left the Bar with as much dignity as she could muster.

So that was what her fine new facial and hair styling did for her – ensured that she was picked up within minutes of leaving the hairdresser's ministrations. What a fool she had been, she told herself furiously.

The bus conductor stopped to chat with her on the way back to Monks Rawley, and by the time she returned to Queensmarket, she was sick of the whole thing. But she couldn't do much about it now. Her hair had been sprayed into shape so that even the wind didn't move it out of place, and her finger-nails sickened her.

What Mrs. Tabb would have to say, she couldn't think.

Mrs. Tabb didn't trust herself to say anything, when Lisa rang the bell to be let in. Her new dress was too tight for her to get in the window again, which was perhaps as well, since Mrs. Tabb had felt the rough edge of Andrew's tongue over that unfortunate incident.

Now she just stared at Lisa, who said briskly, "All right, I know it looks awful, Mrs. Tabb, but it was Dr. Lee who suggested I did it."

That, of course, left Mrs. Tabb speechless. Lisa had a quick tea, snatched her topcoat and went out again, to go to the vicarage.

She walked quickly. She was in no mood for friends to make comments on her altered appearance. Bad enough to have to face Hazel.

She fell back with mock surprise. "What happened to you?" she gasped. "Come on in, before the neighbours talk."

"You haven't got any neighbours, and I've already been picked up in a Bar and flirted with by the bus conductor," Lisa said shortly.

"But that nice little hairdresser in Monks Rawley would never do such a thing," Hazel wailed.

"He didn't get a chance. I didn't like the look of the place. I got a bus to Skegwell. Don't say *why* – it just happened to be the next bus that came along, and anyway, it was a jolly good hairdressers – look at my nails."

"Ugh. Green – I hate those. What did Andrew say?" Hazel shuddered.

"He hasn't seen me yet. He's grappling with the Bricketts' fourth baby."

"Dr. Lee?"

"He was in his room – presumably building up strength to take surgery tonight if Andrew doesn't get back in time."

"Dare I ask what Mrs. Tabb said?"

Lisa laughed mirthlessly. "I'm so sick of what she says that I waded in first and told her Dr. Lee had suggested it. That took the wind out of her sails completely."

"Well, heaven knows what Godfrey Kidman will have to say when he sees what's turned up to teach the twins to bang on his piano."

"I can always alter my mind about that, and go instead with you to the hospital. Your Nigel won't be rude about it."

"Oh, won't he. And don't call him *my* Nigel. And if you don't mind, I think I'd better see him alone tonight. I don't want a witness while I'm shouting at him."

Hazel and Lisa went out in the car soon after that. Hazel said she didn't want her father to get a shock with the sight of Lisa.

"It's a good thing I like you, isn't it," Lisa chuckled. "Still, you're not as blunt as Dinah Gregory. I didn't tell you about that, did I? She met me in a milk bar and she told me Andrew had been in love with his first wife so deeply that he'd never love anyone else and I must have got him on the rebound. What about that?"

Hazel was so angry that she jerked the steering wheel and the car overtaking them let out a blare of his horn that must have been heard for miles. "Look out," Lisa gasped.

"Sorry. Caught me on the wrong foot.

That Dinah Gregory, I ought to have warned you about her. She really is a cat, and Andrew has never seen that side of her. Well, she takes good care of that. They grew up together."

"So he tells me."

"You never told him she said that, did you, Lisa?" Hazel was scandalised.

"Yes, I did actually. We – well, we weren't very pleasant to each other, though it blew over. But I had to get it off my chest because he'd just ticked me off for being out for hours and no-one knew where I was. I was furious. No-one wants me at home and the minute I take myself off, they get mad because they don't know where I am or what I'm doing."

"What did he say to that – or shouldn't I ask?"

"He said I must have thought she said it, but that she said something else."

"Unfortunate, but I'm not surprised. I shouldn't think Andrew would dream of saying anything against her. He's like that with old friends. I should be careful not to accuse any of them."

"That isn't me," Lisa said furiously. "He'd better get used to the idea now as later. Oh, what's the matter with me, talking like that about Andrew? A fine example to anyone unmarried, aren't I? How can one talk about someone in that way, when one – oh, I don't know. I'm just silly about Andrew and it'll always be the same, but I do get mad at him nowadays."

"Did you know him long before you married him?" Hazel asked delicately.

"No, and if you say anything about marrying in haste, I shall tell you pretty smartly that it wasn't like that, either. We had time to get to know each other, and when we were in London we were perfectly happy together. It's only since we came back here that things haven't been quite as harmonious. And you believe me when I say I wouldn't talk like this to anyone else. You're privileged."

"I say, I wish you wouldn't," Hazel said, embarrassed, but pleased with the compliment. "Anyway, here we are at the horrible Kidman twins' house. About Andrew, he's the salt of the earth, you know, but he does have an awful lot to put up with. Always has had. And he's tremendously loyal to his old friends. You just remember that, and tons of luck."

"Tons of luck yourself," Lisa retorted. "And about that nice Nigel of yours, do go easy with him. He likes you a terrible lot, so don't keep slapping him down."

Hazel pulled a face at her and drove off, her cheeks scarlet.

The Kidman children stood side by side while their father delivered a little lecture about being well behaved with their new music teacher and he explained to Lisa that their mother was away looking after a sick relative. Having done that, he showed Lisa the parlour – an old-fashioned room with open folding doors in the middle – and washed his hands of the whole thing. He was a big burly man in rough tweeds, with a enormous meerschaum pipe smoking foully in his mouth all the time he talked. Lisa wondered what he did for a living, and thought he looked a typical farmer.

She settled the children on the long seat before the cottage piano and said, by way of a preliminary skirmish, "Do either of you know anything about playing the piano?" This was always a cautious opening gambit, since Lisa had carefully taught one imp the first four lessons out of the beginner book and then found that the little wretch could play passably well up to Grade III.

The twins spoke at once; the girl said 'yes' and the boy said'no' then they looked at each other, giggled, and both said the opposite.

"Oh, it's going to be like that, is it," Lisa said, with resignation. "All right. I'll take you first, Bernie, for half the lesson. You go away and play, Audrey, and see you come back in fifteen minutes time, or else I shall go."

Audrey appeared to be about to argue, when her brother made a sign with his eyebrows. Lisa wasn't in time to see just what it conveyed, but Audrey went without further argument.

He was a bright boy, so to encourage him, Lisa taught him how to play a little jingle. To come from the piano after the first lesson, able to play something, was always an encouragement and a triumph for the bright but impatient child, Lisa had always found.

The freckled Audrey was back, true to her instructions, in fifteen minutes, but this time Lisa noticed Audrey looked sharply back at something behind the folding doors.

"What is it?" she asked, getting up to go and look.

"Just the cat," Audrey said quickly, "but he's gone now."

Lisa shrugged and let the boy vanish, out to play presumably. She concentrated on his twin for the next quarter of an hour, but the result was less rewarding. Audrey appeared to be giving only half her attention of the lesson.

"What's the matter?" she asked, when she got up to go. "Don't you think you're going to like learning to play, or is it going to be too difficult? Don't be afraid to say."

While the child hesitated, there came a peculiar interruption. From behind the folding door a wheel-chair was pushed.

Audrey scrambled to her feet and spoke to the girl in the chair. "What did you do that for? Dad'll be mad, good and proper. You know that."

"And who is this?" Lisa asked quietly, of Audrey, though she looked at the girl. Her legs were covered by a plaid blanket, and she looked white and frail, but it had been a pretty face once, and the shy smile was very appealing.

"It's our Mollie," Audrey said. "She wanted to go in the garden only our Dad said she'd got to give an eye to us in case we played you up. That's why she was behind the curtains."

"Well, supposing you run off, Audrey, while Mollie and I have a little talk," Lisa suggested gently.

"I can't, can I?" Audrey burst out. She seemed very upset.

"Why not? I won't eat her, will I Mollie?"

Mollie didn't answer. She, too, seemed distressed, now that she had seen Lisa. Lisa remembered that Kidman himself hadn't been able to take his eyes off her face, and he hadn't seemed very pleased.

Audrey said, "She doesn't speak to strangers." She seemed to be desperate about something. "Our Mollie wanted to meet you. She's been listening behind the curtain only — well, you see, our Bernie's in the choir — "

"So that's where I've seen him before.

I thought his face was familiar," Lisa exclaimed.

"I'm trying to tell you, miss. Our Bernie and our Dad thought you were all nice and not like *her*. (Well, I have to tell her, don't I?) Only now you look all different and it's scaring our Mollie."

Mollie tried to get her chair turned round, to escape. Lisa took a look at herself in the mirror over the mantelpiece, and realised with a shock that she was still as the hairdresser in Skegwell had turned her out that afternoon.

"Oh, all this stuff on my face. Don't mind that. I tried it for fun but no-one likes it, so it's going to be washed off. Mollie, I suppose you wouldn't like to be a pupil, too? Or do you play the piano already?" she said, on inspiration.

The girl's face lit for a moment, then she came over shy and couldn't say a word.

"She don't talk to strangers," Audrey said earnestly. "It's since her accident. Do you know about that?" she added doubtfully.

"No. Should I? I haven't been here very long."

Audrey looked relieved. "Doesn't matter," she mumbled.

And then Hazel drove up in her car. She put her finger on the button and blared on a long note.

"I'll go and open the door," Audrey said, and ran. Delighted, no doubt, to be seeing the back of an uncomfortable visitor.

"Mollie, I've got an idea," Lisa said following the escaping wheelchair. "Why don't you sit behind the curtain when I'm giving the twins their lesson and you can hear and try it out for yourself when I'm gone. Have a sort of secret lesson, eh? The twins will show you what they've learnt. Then perhaps one day you'll like to surprise me by showing me what you can do."

Mollie didn't answer, but she had hesitated for a minute in her headlong flight, so perhaps see would consider the proposition. It might take root, have some effect.

Hazel looked thoroughly pleased with herself. "First, did you collect your money? I thought you wouldn't," she said in disgust, as Lisa settled herself in her seat and Hazel drove them away from the Kidman house.

"Well, I forgot. Mr. Kidman vanished after he'd given the twins over to my care. Then there was a girl in a wheelchair appeared at the end of the lesson — "

"Mollie? That's odd. No-one ever sees her nowadays."

"Detailed by their father to watch from behind a curtain and see the twins didn't play up," Lisa said briefly. "What happened to her?"

"I knew it. I knew you'd come up with another awkward question."

"Is it anything to do with us — the Lees, I mean?"

"What made you say that?"

"Well, young Audrey seemed to think I would know about it."

Hazel took her time in answering that. At last, she said, "She was on a pedestrian crossing. That dodgy one at the crossroads in Monks Rawley. You probably noticed it this afternoon."

"Yes. Actually a policeman was trying to sort out a muddle of traffic there."

"Well, Mollie was knocked down on it, and the driver didn't stop."

"Oh, no. Didn't they ever find out who did it?"

"Yes. Of course they did. There were plenty of people about at the time."

"Well, who? Oh, Hazel, you're not going to tell me it was one of the Lees?"

"I'm afraid so," Hazel said grimly. "It was Andrew's half-brother Tobias. Of course, it's all gone and forgotten now. He was forced to go away, of course, and Kidman being who he was, of course, he didn't make too much of a fuss. But the two families had to stump up, by way of compensation. She won't ever walk again."

"What two families?" Lisa asked, not following. She had been thinking about poor Andrew, coming back here with the knowledge that someone's child had been crippled by his own half-brother, when he himself was committed to saving life, not damaging or destroying it.

"The Mawsons, of course," Hazel said, concentrating on her driving. But they were entering the square, and she suddenly realised what she had said. "Now why did I – " she began crossly, then stopped.

"Why should the Mawsons do any such thing?" Lisa inevitably wanted to know. "What had it got to do with them?"

Lisa's heart was thumping, a slow yet increasing tempo. She knew she was going to hear something she didn't want to hear, and she steeled herself to receive the blow.

"Didn't I tell you?" Hazel said, thinking quickly. "They're Kidman's employers. Oh, that was in the days when they were all there, and quite well-off, and they always looked after their employees. It was the natural thing for them to do."

"Very generous of them," Lisa said in surprise, feeling curiously let down, after being led to expect something much more dramatic. "They've had a tough time, one way and another, haven't they, what with the scandal and having to stump up money to cover that up?" she mused. "One of the visitors at the hospital was telling me about it, but she saw her bus go by just when she was getting to the interesting part about it. She'd just started saying about it being the only girl, and the boys naturally covered up, then she just said goodbye and ran. Through some passage or other, to cut it off as it came into the square. Everyone runs when they get to the interesting part of what they were telling me."

Hazel listened to all this in dismay. She had made no attempt to break into that long speech of Lisa's, because for one thing Lisa rarely said so much at a time, and for another she was overcome with how near Lisa had arrived at finding out all the things that Andrew didn't want her to know. Hazel's father wouldn't be pleased when he heard about this. He had been telling her only that morning how anxious Andrew had been about Lisa stumbling over so much old history. Apparently Andrew had been hoping that sleeping dogs would be allowed to lie.

"Yes, well, here we are," Hazel said, pulling up outside The Old House. "And do you realise that you haven't yet asked me how I got on, visiting Nigel?"

Hazel's face was in the shadow cast by the street lamp. In this part of Queensmarket they were still the old romantic-looking gas lamps. The square hadn't yet been provided with the modern-looking cement arc lamps that the High

Street had. The gas lamps threw wavering uncertain shadows, with the aid of the nearby trees. Hazel might be laughing or embarrassed: Lisa couldn't be sure.

"I'm sorry, and I wanted to hear about it so much. Go on, tell me."

"Not on your life – not now, Lisa. You get into that house and wipe that muck off your face before Andrew see you."

"That reminds me. The Kidman children had something to say about it, and it wasn't very flattering," Lisa chuckled. "Apparently their father had seen me in church (without the efforts of Pierre and Chantelle, of course) and young Bernie is in the choir and had apparently passed me as an innocuous old music teacher. They all got the shock of their lives this afternoon. I'd forgotten about it till I saw myself in the glass."

Hazel blinked. She could very well imagine that Godfrey Kidman wouldn't be pleased to see that Lisa was falling into the ways of others who hadn't pleased him in the past. "Well, just go indoors and have a wash," she said, almost pushing Lisa out of the car.

All Hazel wanted to do was to get to

the vicarage and use the telephone. Call up Andrew and warn him of how much Lisa had managed to find out. That, she considered was urgent.

Lisa, knowing nothing of what was in her friend's mind, hurried in, expecting to find Andrew fuming because he didn't know where she was. Then she remembered she had left him a note on the desk in the surgery, on which she had added the bit about the house in London. Her heart lifted, as she thought of how nice it would be for just Andrew and herself to go up to London on his next day off.

She could hear old Dr. Lee talking, and she stood still, trying to decide where he was, and who he had got with him. She hoped it was one of his Chess-playing friends so that she could be sure he would be fully occupied long enough to leave her for a while alone with Andrew.

Andrew's voice, however, answered his father. "I don't like it, but I can't think what else to do," he was saying. He sounded so worried.

His father sounded impatient. "You've got it handed to you on a plate, my boy.

Why hedge about it? The girl wants to go back to her house. Let her go, then. It's a godsend at this particular unhappy moment — doesn't sound like an excuse to get rid of her, especially as she's raised the point to you herself."

Lisa felt sick. They were talking about her, and that note she had left Andrew. They were going to send her back to No. 19, and pretend it was because she had asked about it, when all the time they just wanted to see the back of her.

She went quietly out of the house again, sick at heart. She heard the telephone ring, and Andrew's voice answer it, but she was too far away to hear what he said, or that it was Hazel he was talking to.

She stood half in the shadows of a big bush, in the front garden. The square was quiet, the shops all closed. A light was in an upper window of Martin Biddell's. He would be doing the daily crossword puzzle. There was a light across the square in one of Zillie Denner's windows. He would be listening to his classical records. Hazel would be in the vicarage superintending her father's evening meal, telling him about her visit to the hospital and the progress of their organist. Those people were all happy, secure in their place in life. But she, Lisa Willard – no, Lisa Lee now, was not secure, not really wanted, anywhere.

How was it that Nigel loved Queensmarket so much that he couldn't leave it? Quite suddenly Lisa hated it. Hated the restless flicking of the light in the lighthouse. Hated the ever present rumble and crashing of the sea, the moaning of the wind, the cry of the gulls. She wanted London so badly that it hurt.

She was just about to turn to go back into the house and tell Andrew this, when a man let himself out of the front door. She had seen him before. She racked her brains to know where, and as he stood there casually lighting a match to his cigarette, the sudden illumination of his face told her where she had seen him. He was the man who had tried to pick her up in the Honey Bar that afternoon.

11

SHE stood stock still, hoping he wouldn't see her. She didn't want him to speak to her. Now she began to dimly understand how it was his face had seemed familiar. It was her guess that it was one of Andrew's half brothers.

It wasn't possible for him not to see her if he continued out to the gate, but suddenly the door behind him opened and Mrs. Tabb stood there. On her face was a queer softened look that was near to tears. Lisa was astonished. She had always considered that Mrs. Tabb had such a hard face.

"Come in, Master Toby, do," she said softly, so that Lisa barely caught the words. "You know the doctor doesn't want you to be seen. Come in, do, to my kitchen and I'll make you — "

What she was going to make for him was lost in a soft mumble as he turned laughing and put an arm round her waist. They went in together.

What on earth was going on? Lisa turned and ran out of the front garden. How could she go back in that house, if they had one of the brothers there and hoped to send her away? That, she supposed, was the reason. But how long did they think they could keep Andrew's wife in ignorance of all this?

She walked through the passage to the rough end of the shore to the lighthouse and the fisherman's cottages. She didn't like this end of the shore and it matched her mood. Besides, she wanted to think. It struck her then that Andrew hadn't really wanted her to come here, and having brought her here, he had probably hoped she would not like it, and would ask to go back to London. In fact, he had almost said that if she wanted to stay in London she could while he came here and helped his father. But for how long?

Lisa walked for an hour until she realised she was cold and hungry and rather tired. It had been a full day.

She went back because there was nothing else she could do. She found the front door was half open and as she walked up the path she heard Mrs. Tabb call out,

"Here she is, doctor – coming now."

Old Dr. Lee came out into the hall and stood waiting for her. He stared at Lisa, getting the full blast of the new face and hairdo for the first time.

"Have you no consideration, girl?" he roared. "We've been worried sick. The vicarage rang to say you'd be in any minute. Where did you go after that?"

"For a walk," she said, scowling at him. She was in no mood to have Dr. Lee throwing a tantrum for her benefit. "Hadn't you better not get upset, Dr. Lee? I thought you were still far from well."

"What have you done to yourself?" he demanded, looking her up and down as if, she thought resentfully, she were a stupid patient who had got worse through flagrantly disobeying his advice.

"I did what you suggested, Dr. Lee. I went to a hairdressers and got things done to myself. I'm sorry if you don't like it."

Then Andrew came hurrying in. "Where on earth have you been, Lisa, all this time? I've been looking for you."

"What did the vicar want to telephone

about me for?" she asked.

"He didn't," Andrew said, and then caught his father's frown. "Never mind about that. Where have you been?"

"Walking on the shore. Thinking. Andrew, I don't like being here. I've tried, but I want to go back to my own house."

Father and son exchanged glances, and Andrew's anger subsided. "Well, it might be arranged," he said tiredly. "Let's go into the sitting-room and talk about it. And what, in heaven's name, have you done to yourself?"

"That's what everyone keeps saying to me and I'm getting rather bored with it. Let's talk about me going back to London."

Andew stood staring at her. She could hear Dr. Lee stumping back to his room. Mrs. Tabb had gone to the kitchen. There was no sound anywhere of that other man, but Lisa thought she could feel his presence somewhere, and he was all part of the things she didn't like about Queensmarket.

"All right, let's talk about that," Andrew agreed at last. "When would you like to go back?"

"You're not putting up much of a fight to try and make me change my mind," she said, with a suspicious wobble in her voice.

"Please, Lisa, we're both tired. Let's keep this discussion practical, shall we? Either you stay here and be reasonable and not worry me with these unexplained absences or you go back to your own house. I don't mind which, but do let's have done with all this nonsense."

"You wouldn't mind if I went back for good?" she asked.

"Let's say a month," he allowed. "In that time I should know what my own position is. I doubt if I can keep up this pace much longer myself, and my father does seem better. We'll see, we'll see. Meantime — "

"Meantime one of us ought to find out about Mrs. Cobb and if she's still holding the fort," Lisa said, with a gasp. "You won't believe this, but I'd forgotten all about her."

"Well, I hadn't," he said shortly. "I've been on the telephone twice, and the delay is still dragging on. I gather she's getting anxious herself. She cabled her son and got no reply. So perhaps it might be as well if you did go back."

She nodded miserably. This wasn't the way she had wanted it.

She got up and went and put her arms round his neck. "Don't be cross with me. Hazel did drop me at the house, but – well, I got the urge to go for a walk on the shore and I heard your voice and your father's and I thought if you were both talking, you wouldn't miss me. And I must have walked further than I meant to."

He absently held her, stroking the back of her head, but it was all stiff and set and unfamiliar and he took his hand away and held her off. "What in the world possessed you to do that to your hair?" he asked again. "I don't like it."

"Your father didn't like it as it was before," she pointed out crossly. "No-one seems to like whatever I try to do."

"Lisa, you're getting the oddest ideas about people. You said Dinah Gregory made the most unpleasant remark to you. I've seen her today and she says it wasn't like that at all. She seemed rather amused, but I wasn't amused."

"Andrew, you never told her what I told you?"

"I certainly did. I meant to get to the bottom of it."

"Oh, Andrew, you don't find out the truth from women by just asking them outright for it," she cried.

"I'm only a simple man. I don't understand the wiles of women or any of their nonsense. All I ask is to be allowed to get on with my job, without all this extraneous anxiety and awareness of the undercurrents all around me. Can't you understand that, Lisa?"

"Yes, I think I can," she said slowly. "But I can tell you this; things will never be the same again between us if you don't clear things up — all the things I want to know about, all the secrets, the things other people know, which gives them the power to form a solid bloc against me and force you and me apart."

"It isn't as easy as you make it sound, Lisa. All right, I could sit down and tell you everything you want to know, but would you be any happier, I wonder?"

"Try me, Andrew, try me," she pleaded.

"No. It's too a big risk. You might

shrink away from me altogether and I couldn't bear that."

"Is it something you've done, then? You couldn't do anything bad, Andrew."

"Don't be childish, Lisa. Who said it was bad? But things need not be bad to be unpalatable, disturbing. And who said it was what I'd done? No, I meant other people, people belonging to me, and with whom I'm involved. Every one of us is involved with others, and no-one can extricate himself entirely from the mistakes of others. It might even be a word or a look – a thought, even – that promoted the act on someone else's part. Who can say? I'm not perfect – I've never pretended to be. It may well be that my very impatience started all this train of events – I don't know. But I want you kept out of it, Lisa."

"If only we'd never come here," she fretted. "If only we could turn back the clock."

"No. No, never say that, Lisa. No-one can do that, and if they could, it would be no different. I'm a fatalist. Things are out of our hands."

"Then if that is your belief, why are

you trying to keep me from getting involved with all this mystery? If you're a fatalist you should realise that no matter how you try to keep me from knowing, I shall stumble on the truth somehow and get involved."

"That's why I want you to go back," he said, nodding. "Back to your own house, in your own street, where I believe you will be happy, and as soon as I can, I'll come to you."

There was no moving him from that decision. He kissed her and then inevitably the telephone rang and he had to go out.

If there was a stranger in that house, Lisa couldn't imagine where he had been hidden. There was no evidence of him by way of shaving kit or toothbrushes in the bathroom. The spare rooms had that empty look that belonged to them, their doors standing wide as always. No strange hat or umbrella adorned the grim-looking hall-stand.

But it was a mystery Lisa had little time to dwell on, for she was packed off on the London train the next day. She had only time for a hasty flick round saying goodbye to Zillie, Martin, and Hazel. An unsatisfactory goodbye visit to each of them, for both Zillie and Martin were involved with customers at the time and Hazel was in an argument with two of the voluntary helpers about who had made an arrangement which displeased them both.

Andrew had promised that he would see to the matter of her music pupils, or ask Hazel to do it. He promised to explain to everyone why she had had to return to London so soon. He promised the earth, she suspected, simply to see the back of her without any more of those tiresome questions of hers.

It was cold for the time of the year. Lisa was glad to be back. As the grey tenements began to close in on her, Lisa felt as if she were entering a friendly land. Flat dirty brick work and curtainless windows were infinitely preferable to her than a windswept shore and sand dunes peppered with spears of whitish grass, bowed perpetually before the wind from the North Sea. She shivered as she thought of it. And not to feel the lighthouse like a baleful eye opening and closing above her all the time was bliss, sheer bliss.

But there the bliss ended, for on her arrival at No. 19 she found Mrs. Cobb in a dreadful state.

The Smiths were with her. "It's her son. He died, in a horse accident. And now she can't go out there. There's no-one to go to."

Andrew and his fatalistic outlook rushed back on Lisa. What would he say to this example of it? A prepared trip to the extent of passage paid and everything sold up, and now . . . nothing.

Lisa did her best to comfort Mrs. Cobb, but she was a stranger, knowing little of Mrs. Cobb's background. All she could think of to say was, "Won't you go on living here, then? It's your home as long as you want it."

"But it's your place, dear," Mrs. Cobb protested. "What will you do when you and your husband want to come back?"

"I'm back," Lisa said quietly. "I've come back for a month at least. I might stay for always. I shan't want to be here on my own."

"But what about your husband, dear?" Mrs. Cobb insisted.

"I don't suppose you'll find him in the way at the week-ends – that's if he comes," Lisa said. "He wants to stay and help his father but I couldn't stand it. I didn't like the place."

Mrs. Cobb nodded sagely. "Once a Londoner, always a Londoner. That's the way of it. It's been worrying me, to tell you the truth. What if I couldn't stand Australia, I kept asking myself. It's such a long way from home. Maybe it's judgment, this, for me not really wanting to go."

"No, no, I'm sure it isn't," Lisa hastened to assure her. "Think how much more awful it would have been if you'd arrived out there to find you were alone among strangers when it happened. And have to come back again, to nowhere. Now you've got a roof over your head and you've got me."

"Yes. It does make a difference. It's the shock. I expect. Not knowing where I was going or what I was going to do. I'd sunk everything into going out there. Sold up everything, and at my time of life – "

Lisa nodded. "At any time of life it's

bad to be uprooted, if you don't really want to go."

To help take Mrs. Cobb's mind off her loss, Lisa slipped into the habit of telling her all that happened since she had left No. 19. The telling of it eased Lisa's heartache, and helped her to see it from a fresh angle, and Mrs. Cobb's remarks added new thought to the problem, at times.

"This here Zillie Denner. That was a funny sort of remark to make about the grand piano, I must say. What's he like? Is he a man you can trust, dear?"

"Oh, yes he's nice. He hasn't got much of his Austrian accent left, and he has nice manners and a very sincere look in his eyes. I got the feeling he had let that slip out, but he kept a watch over his tongue afterwards, and it tended to spoil the nice times we had together, because he couldn't feel free to chat without running the risk of letting something else slip."

"And this Biddell, the chemist. He's a young chap, you say?"

"Yes, he's very nice, but he always seems to be comparing me with that woman. Why do you suppose they won't just tell me what she was like and have done with it?"

"Seems to me they have, duck," Mrs. Cobb said slowly. "Now, this German – well, Austrian, then. This Zillie Denner. (What a name!) He says she had to have that piano so much, they raised hell to get it, and the poor owner had to sell it because he needed the money. Yet he says she wasn't a music lover. So we know she was fond of her own way and they were so fond of her, they pampered her and gave it to her. Right?"

Lisa nodded dumbly.

"Then the old housekeeper admits she's tall. So she's tall and pampered. And this organist chap says she was so beautiful, that's all he can think of. She must have been careful of her looks to spend so much money on hairdressing and make-up and clothes and I don't know what. Did she drive her own car?"

"I don't know that. Wait a minute, though. Hazel (that's the vicar's daughter) seemed to expect me to own one and drive it, and when I said I didn't, she hastily had a think and then offered to drive me around in her car. It was a new thing, though; I could tell it hadn't happened before."

Lisa threw herself into discussing it with Mrs. Cobb because she could see that it was helping the little woman, but she couldn't give her the complete picture because of admitting the truth about the sleeping arrangements. That much she had to keep to herself for pride's sake, for in her heart she felt that Andrew was carrying devotion too far, if he really thought she would sleep better on her own because of the night calls, especially as she slept through any noise. No, the truth was pressing in on her; he had loved that other woman so much, this new marriage just wasn't going to hold. It was the thin edge of the wedge, that sleeping arrangement.

"Mind you," Mrs. Cobb said, thinking, "there is a little matter of where all the money came from for her car, her clothes, her hair appointments and I don't know what. Did she have money of her own, d'you know?"

"No, I don't. I don't even know who she was before she married Andrew, but his great friend Carmichael Mawson called her Tressida."

"Yes, I'm not sure I like the sound of that chap. D'you know what I reckon? I reckon he was in love with the doctor's first wife. There you are. What about that for an idea?"

"Carmichael? Oh, but he's so nice. Oh, he wouldn't steal another man's wife, I'm sure," Lisa protested, shocked.

"Who said anything about stealing? A chap can love another man's wife from a distance, can't he? But it could be noticed by the husband."

Noticed by the husband. Or by the husband's father, or his housekeeper.

"There's another thing," Mrs. Cobb went on. "He didn't want to go with you into the house. Said something about easier to get out of the square. Well, you know best about that, of course, but in my opinion, if he was such a great friend of your husband's, dear, and there hadn't been any trouble with the first wife, how is it he can leave his farm to take dogs to people and sit in their sitting-room chatting and then take home someone and sit chatting in the car, and yet he hasn't got time to look in on his old friends?"

"Yes, I wondered about that, too," Lisa said. "But *Carmichael.* He's so nice. I wouldn't have thought it of him."

She thought a minute. "But if that were true, surely the old doctor wouldn't cherish her memory so much that he hates the sight of me? Surely he'd think – ?"

"Well, no, not if it was all on the side of this Mawson chap," Mrs. Cobb objected.

"Poor Carmichael, and after all that trouble in his own family, too. Some people have it all go wrong."

"Maybe he turned to the doctor's lady for solace, as they say, because he was fed-up with things going wrong at home, eh?" Mrs. Cobb suggested. "Then there's this vet. She came right out and said a few things, didn't she? Mind you, without seeing that little madam, I can't quite make up my mind about her. Something about it doesn't ring true. If she wants to make you miserable, it sounds like jealousy, but why be jealous of you, if what we think about the first wife is right? I should watch that vet. woman, if I were you, dear."

12

BACK in her own room again, Lisa waited for the healing that she had expected this trip to London would bring.

Even the weather was more kind here. Waking in the morning, she was free from the constraint that the sight of the lighthouse had brought. It was sheer delight to hear cheeky London sparrows on the apple tree outside, instead of the discontented shriek of the gulls and the low worrying moan of the wind from the sea.

Funny, she thought, how the old sounds meant so much. The ones she waited for, from six thirty onwards: the clonk-clonk of the paper boy up the little front path and the special big *clonk* of the papers landing on the floor, skidding as always on the polished lino to land up against the little grandmother clock, and that always emitted a protesting clang of chime against chime. Old Lazarus, the milkman, who had a game leg, and stumped skip-and-go-hop halfway up the path to where the milk box was kept, with its shutter, to guard the tinfoil caps of the bottles against the marauding tits.

None of these things were heard at The Old House. Mrs. Tabb's influence made everything run smoothly, to a colourless perfection. She wouldn't have allowed a clock like the one in Lisa's sitting-room to miss a beat at ten thirty, night and morning, and let out a noisy *whir-r-r-r*. Mrs. Tabb would have taken that to the clock repairer in the Square at once.

Inevitably Lisa was approached by mothers of old pupils, who had heard she was back again, however temporarily. She found she was wrestling with Bertie's tone deafness and Sybil's spasmodic brilliance again; Mick Warren's steady plodding and Mary Jones' show-off tricks. Mrs. Cobb liked to come and sit in the same room, listening to the lesson while she did the mending for both of them, or her knitting – that eternal knitting. When she had finished the salmon pink cardigan for herself, she said, she would do a lime green jersey for Lisa. "Knitting fair sets the nerves down," Mrs. Cobb was fond of saying.

It was at Mrs. Cobb's instigation that Lisa should go out somewhere fresh every day. "Don't worry about me, dear. I shall be all right, just knowing you'll be back later and in the house all night with me. It's someone to prepare an evening meal for and keep the place dusted for. Wonderful what a difference having to do for someone does make to a body."

Lisa said she didn't know where to go, and wouldn't admit for worlds that she had lost the habit of pleasing herself. In Queensmarket a new pattern of duties had presented themselves, beginning with Hazel and the new pupils, and chasing the disturbing ghost of Tressida, finding out what she could about her, so that each new day had been a challenge. Here the ghost of Tressida couldn't reach her, but it had left her curiously empty. Andrew wouldn't have any need to worry any more about whether she was late in or not, because she wasn't there. Mrs. Tabb wouldn't have cause to grumble about Lisa being late for meals or fetching her to the front door. Old Dr. Lee no longer had cause to look at her with displeasure; his days could be spent in blissful relief from a disappointing new daughter-in-law.

So Lisa told herself bitterly that morning, the fourth since she had left Queensmarket, and the telling gave her no pleasure.

"Look at you, dear," Mrs. Cobb scolded. "Too much time on your hands. Your next music lesson's not till seven o'clock tonight. Why don't you take yourself to the Tower of London, eh? How long ago is it since you went to the Zoo? What about feeding the pigeons in Trafalgar Square?"

"Not since I've been grown up," Lisa said, answering the first part of all that. "And I think I should feel rather a fool going to the Zoo all by myself."

"Well, how about pleasing Mrs. Smith (who's been so kind to me) and taking her youngest off her hands for the day? That'd be a real act of charity because that boy's a mort too lively for a party in middle years. Unless, of course, you don't care for young children?"

Heartache claimed Lisa as she thought

of how much she longed for a child of her own. "All right, I'll do that," she said.

"You go along now and see Mrs. Smith and I'll make you some nice sandwiches and put in some tomatoes and milk and apples and a bit of chocolate, and you can buy the little nipper some ice-cream when you're getting yourself a nice hot cuppa."

That, Lisa reflected, was giving Mrs. Cobb something good to do; something she adored. Packing food and seeing other people off. "I suppose you wouldn't like to come, too?" Lisa asked her.

"No, duck, my days of tramping round gawping at animals and beefeaters and pigeons are over. It's me for me feet up and a nice listen to the wireless while I have my bit of lunch."

A day at the Zoo. What would she have thought, four days ago, Lisa asked herself, if she could have peeped into the near future? Young Roddy was almost five, a big boy for his age, and he asked questions about everything, nonstop. She gave herself up to answering him, if only to take her mind off Andrew, wondering what he was doing, and whether there had been anything in Mrs. Cobb's warning about the vet. – a girl she had never even seen.

They had a camera with them. It was Roddy's – a workmanlike little box camera that he insisted on using for every animal until he ran out of films. Lisa bought him another film and he took some pictures of her while she wasn't looking. At last she decided it was time to eat their lunch.

"Let's go out into the park and have it, shall we?" she suggested. Her feet were aching, and it was a busy and rather noisy day at the Zoo. She supposed it was because of the unusually hot weather after a long chilly wet spell.

"No, let's stay here. On this seat," Roddy persuaded.

"What's so special about this seat?" she wanted to know.

"It's at the end. You can't go any further, can you?"

"No, that's true. Is it important?"

"Yes. Then we can find out if that man has really been following us. Like in the pictures on telly, or if it was because he was going the same way as us and couldn't help it."

"Which man, you idiot child?" she laughed.

"There. Standing watching us behind the fat lady. Look, the one in the green hat, with his coat over his shoulder. That's like my big brother stands, when he's looking at a girl and making up his mind to speak to her. At least, that's what my sister says he's doing."

Lisa was no longer listening to the child's precocious conversation. She was staring unbelievingly at the young man who now emerged boldly from the shelter of the fat lady staring up at the parrots and walked towards Lisa and young Roddy.

"Oh, no, it can't be," she whispered in horror to herself.

"Do you know him then?" Roddy asked with interest. He was used to situations like this. When he was out with his big sister and a young man came up to them Roddy was usually given a shilling to amble off and buy sweets or ice lollies. He looked expectantly at Lisa and then at the newcomer. But they both ignored the child. They had eyes only for each other, and Lisa's eyes were brooding, vaguely scared. This was the man in the Honey Bar, the man who had been at The Old House, and who had been persuaded to go into the kitchen out of sight with Mrs. Tabb.

"Hello, there," he said easily, coming to a halt in front of Lisa. He had bold Italian good looks, none of the fine features and distinguished air of Andrew, but rather a Continental truculence and charm and a hint of mischief rolled into one. "It's Mrs. Andrew, isn't it?"

"Her name's Lisa," Roddy put in, trying to draw attention to himself.

Tobias Lee looked down at him. "I know, chum," he said easily, doing what Roddy had confidently hoped and expected he would. "Here, here's a bob. Know what to do with it? Scram, then, and don't hurry back."

"Don't send him away," Lisa gasped. "He isn't five yet, and I'm responsible for him."

"Go on. That kid knows his whereabouts. If ever a brat was sitting up begging to be paid to clear out, that one was. So it's *Lisa.*"

Lisa tried to get up to go after Roddy, but it was difficult. Their clothes and the lunch basket were spread out all round them, and Tobias held on to her wrist. She didn't want to make a scene here, and anyway, she could see Roddy confidently lining up in a queue of small fry at the ice-cream stall. She gave it up.

"All right, so you're Andrew's half-brother, and you were at The Old House the night before I left. How did you find out where I was? They were all trying to pretend that no-one else was in the house."

"And how right they were," he said mockingly. "I was in the old stables, behind Martin Biddell's place. Oh, yes he was in the plot, too. Everyone knew I was back, I shouldn't wonder. Much to the embarrassment of the inmates of The Old House." He chuckled. "You know, you're quite something, aren't you? Not so disturbingly beautiful as Tressida, but interesting, very. In a quite different way. Wonder what possessed that absurd half-brother of mine to let you back to London all by yourself? You need someone to look after you, and I'm your man."

Lisa disliked him so much that she was sure it must show all over her. "You are not my man," she said clearly.

"Oh? Is that all you are going to say?" His eyes glinted "I expected quite a speech. An indignant one, about being a married woman and Andrew wouldn't like it, and neither would the old man, and what would people say, and moreover, what would people think? People, lord-love-them, have a habit of thinking far more about other people's affairs than they do about their own, and you haven't even mentioned this tiresome habit of theirs."

"I said all I needed to say," she told him coldly.

"You don't like me, I do believe," he marvelled.

"That's right, I don't like you," Lisa said.

"Now I wonder if you worked that out all by yourself (which would make you much more interesting than most girls) or whether those self-same people, lord-love-them, have been *talking*."

"I wish you'd leave us alone," she said, trying to get up. "I don't know how you knew where to find me – ”

"Simple. Mrs. Tabb told me. You're not going to get very far with her, you know. Nor with most people in Queensmarket. You see, Tressida was there first, and claimed their allegiance. No-one could adore Tressida and have any room for anyone else. But you've heard that already, no doubt?"

He was staring hard into her troubled brown eyes, reading there the unhappiness and doubt before she could decently draw the veil over them.

"Yes, I thought so. What did they tell you about her?"

"They told me about you, which was enough. How you ran down a child on a crossing. She's fourteen now, and has no hope of walking. She spends her life in a wheelchair, too shy to speak to anyone. Hiding, in the shelter of her own home."

He looked taken aback at that, then he laughed shortly. "Get the picture right, for heaven's sake, Lisa, love. I was certainly driving the car, but it was hardly my fault. The lady who was with me had to choose that moment to start messing about with the scarf over her hair, and the end blew right across my face. I couldn't see a damned thing. In an open car with the rain pelting down, it just needs that sort of thing to happen, and there you are. The kid happened to be on the crossing, and there you are."

"But you didn't even stop," Lisa accused.

"Oh, dear, you don't know Queensmarket very well, do you? We are the Lees, ducky, who have lived there for generations. One does not get discovered knocking people down in Monks Rawley in a car that contains a lady to whom one is not married. Someone else was married to her, so – for her sake as much as mine, I tried to beat it. Why not? I could see the kid getting up in my mirror, I knew I'd hit something but not all that bad." He narrowed his eyes. "Stop looking at me in judgment, Lisa. I didn't know I'd hurt that girl enough to make her a cripple for life, so help me. Now can we talk about something else?"

"Yes, such as me collecting that child and taking him elsewhere."

"Had enough of the Zoo? Me, too,

Where shall we go now?"

"Not you, Tobias. I just don't want to be with you," she said.

He made the sketch of a salute, and sauntered away, and she was left trembling all over from the impact. Why had he followed her? Had she really got rid of him? And was his version of that accident true, or not?

Roddy came back, looking disappointed. "Why did he go? I liked him."

"He has other things to do," Lisa told the child.

By the time they got back to the boy's home, he had collected a soiled bandage round one knee with an imposing red mark across it, where he had fallen down some steps; he had a dirty face and a raving hunger, in spite of his having had most of Lisa's share of the food. He was jubilant. "I've had a super sort of day," he told his mother. "Can I go again?"

"You must see if Mrs. Lee asks you," his mother said, and began to thank Lisa.

"Her name's Lisa and she said I could, and I hope she brings her boy-friend because he's super and he gave me a bob to go away and leave them alone."

Lisa's heart sank. She had hoped that Tobias wouldn't be mentioned. She hadn't intended to even speak of him to Mrs. Cobb. Now, to judge by Mrs. Smith's startled look it would get to Mrs. Cobb anyway.

"It was only my husband's brother," she said hastily. "I didn't even know he was in London, and it's doubtful if I shall run into him again. I hope you didn't mind Roddy being allowed to spend his money on ice-cream."

In spite of Lisa's protests to Mrs. Cobb earlier on that she didn't want to go out by herself, Lisa felt that another day with the lively Roddy would be too nerve-wearing to make it worthwhile, so she went to London the next time by herself.

It was three days later; a greyish morning that promised to turn out fine in the afternoon. Lisa decided to go round the big shops. Window-shopping was not a thing one could indulge in satisfactorily in Queensmarket. Lisa had discovered that one soon knew the shops by heart, and almost always ran into someone who knew one and wanted to gossip.

She spent a glorious couple of hours before lunch, and bought new shoes – the sort she couldn't hope to get elsewhere. After lunch she went to feed the pigeons, because Mrs. Cobb had set her heart on it.

She had stopped looking over her shoulder now. At first, she had been inclined to think she had seen Tobias. Now she felt sure she was mistaken, and walked lightheartedly down the Strand and through one of the little streets down to the river.

A water-bus was almost ready to start, so she bought her ticket to Tower Pier, but there were gulls on the river, and they reminded her of Queensmarket, and to her intense annoyance tears stung the back of her eyes. She didn't know why she felt like that. She certainly didn't like the place any more than when she had been there, but she missed it, and missed the new life there.

Furious with herself for slipping into what Nigel had called 'the state of having been bitten by the Queensmarket bug', she saw a man's hand come forward to grasp the rail by her side, and a familiar voice said mockingly, "Don't tell me you're homesick for The Old House?"

She looked up to find Tobias beside her.

"Now don't tell me it's a coincidence, Lisa, me being here, because I couldn't bear that."

"Why are you following me, and how did you know where to find me?" she burst out.

"Dear girl, I called for you this morning at your house, and just missed you, so I thought it might be fun to see where you were bound for, all on your own. Besides, I hadn't anything better to do than trail after you while you examined nylon frillies etc."

She coloured, as he had expected her to do. "I like a girl who can still blush. You have a lot of assets that your predecessor hadn't."

"I don't want to hear about her."

"Oh, yes, you do. Or else you wouldn't go around asking everyone about her."

"How do you know I did?"

"Old Tabb told me. And don't ask me

how the old girl knows. She has her spies all over the place."

"You miss the point," Lisa said coldly. "I do want to know about her, naturally. But not from you. I want nothing to do with you."

"That means you find me fascinating and feel you shouldn't. That's where I differ so much from my brother Quentin. Have you heard about Quentin? Old Quentin really was the end. And all because they hadn't succeeded in teaching him as a child the difference between the two little words 'mine' and 'yours'."

"You mean – he was a thief?" Lisa was scandalised, unbelieving.

Tobias chuckled delightedly. "What a strait-laced way of looking at things. All black or white. No, my dear, I wouldn't say he was a thief. A thief creeps in by night and just takes. My brother Quentin borrowed, in broad daylight, and gave quite a lot in exchange – only alas, few other people took such a broad view of his activities."

Lisa willed herself not to be tempted to ask this man to tell her all the things she wanted to know. It was not his place to tell her those things. It was Andrew's place. She said, "Well, he doesn't sound a very nice person to me, and neither do you, and I just wish you'd leave me alone."

They were pulling into Tower Pier. The wharves had given place to the great whitish-grey hulk of the Tower of London. Its green turf surround looked brilliant in the sudden sunshine. Even the grey waters of the Thames looked inviting, with the hurting splashes of sunshine dappling the surface. A little police launch chugged importantly by. It should have been a wonderful day.

Lisa hunched her shoulders angrily as she got off, and tried not to mind the touch of Tobias's hand on her arm, ostensibly helping her.

He wore that hat at such a rakish angle, it was at once amusing and impudent. Like the whole of his person. Girls getting off the water-bus looked him over approvingly and he acknowledged their glances with a pleased, half-inviting cock of one eyebrow. It was Tobias. He just couldn't help it, she thought, ruefully, and it occurred to her then how much

Andrew must have deplored having such a relative. How irritated Andrew must have been, that Fate had dealt him such a stroke of bad luck, for this was the very type of young man that Andrew abhorred most.

She saw Andrew more clearly then than she had ever seem him before. How could Tobias, walking easily by her side, chatting knowledgeably yet half cynically about the Tower and its past history, know that Lisa was putting herself in Andrew's shoes, and aching for all the time he might have been spending at the work he loved in the path. lab. at his old hospital, when he was caught by duty and circumstances in Queensmarket, in his father's practice, with the irritations of every day coupled with the anxiety of his relatives, his past, and Lisa's own reactions to the gossip of local people?

They followed the beefeater guide dutifully until there was a suitable moment to slip the party, on a dark stairway. Trust Tobias to find a way, Lisa thought, in frustration.

"I'd rather stay with the main party," she said coldly.

"Rubbish. I can tell you the story of the Tower much better than the guide can. Look down here," and he forced her to poke her head through a doorway that was barricaded by cross beams of wood.

"No. Let me get back. It goes down for miles," she gasped.

"No, just a floor or two. One keeps happening on these places. I suppose they'll brick it up or something. Want to know what happened there, centuries ago? That was where the Princess Michaela was imprisoned."

"Michaela. There was no such person," Lisa said sharply.

"You couldn't have read the same guide book that I mugged up," he said, outrageously rolling his eyes so that she was hard put not to laugh at him. "The point is, the poor lady was fighting hard against falling in love with her gaoler. He was less uncouth than most and the devil of a fellow. Well, she fought against it until . . . what d'you think happened?"

"She was saved by having to go to the block – if she ever existed," Lisa said tartly.

"No, she succumbed to his charms, and

he got her out of the Tower dressed as his old mother, and he took her away on horseback to live a madly exciting and wicked life with him, only the poor lady contracted smallpox and that was the end of her, as they say in the best nursery rhymes. Come to think of it, she wasn't smart enough. She could have succumbed to his passion before, and then she might have escaped the pox and him too, for a better chap. The whole point is, she was swooning with love from the start, and the ridiculous creature fought against it. Are you going to be like the Princess Adeline?"

"You said her name was Michaela."

"Ah, well, what's in a name? Kiss me, and see how she felt. Same place, different time. Not much in it."

She struggled against him, feeling an insidious charm that she disliked with every ounce of her being. "Let me go, you fool – there's another party coming up."

Tobias shrugged, laughing. "Not to worry. What's a kiss? It's not the kiss but the way the lady reacts to the thought of it, that counts," and he followed her down the stairs without attempting to take her arm.

She was trembling all over. How on earth could she get rid of him? Only by going straight back to Mrs. Cobb, she supposed, and staying there. It was outrageous to think that the much longed for visit to London should be spoilt like this, by the very person she had been sent away to escape.

Now he held her arm, as if he sensed that she was thinking in terms of getting away from him. He was laughing, talking, apparently being the entertaining companion, but all the time his eyes were making love to her, so that her face was hot all the time.

"You know, you really are a sweetie," he murmured into her ear, as they stood on the deck of the returning water-bus. "How did you like the Tower?"

"I didn't. I hated it, thanks to you being there. I never want to even think of the place again, which is a pity, because I was looking forward to it. Haven't you anything better to do than tag along annoying me?"

"If I could be convinced that I really

was annoying you, then I would certainly find something better to do," he said slowly and purposefully.

"How can I show you more pointedly that I hate you being near me?" she burst out.

That was fortunately lost in a sudden blast of a hooter near at hand. She could see, but not hear, Tobias laughing.

"Ah," he said, "but you see, that is no proof that I am annoying you. In that state you might well suddenly capitulate and be full of love for me. Now, now, don't explode. You'll do yourself a mischief if you get so steamed up. Really, old Andrew does acquire the oddest wives."

"What d'you mean by that?"

"Well, take you, for instance. You keep me dangling by pretending you don't like me. Oh, but no matter how you protest, I can see it's so. Now, take the other one . . . ah, that rouses your interest, doesn't it? Now Tressida was different. She didn't ever make the mistake of being unfaithful, either, but she beckoned a chap on. There are some who might say that she wasn't being anything but her natural self, but, well, a chap knows. The girl beckoned and repulsed and drove a chap mad. But to think of poor old sobersides Andrew picking wives like that."

Lisa was bewildered. The more she heard of the late Tressida Lee, the more she was puzzled.

"How did she die?" she asked him.

"Oh, dear, haven't they told you? Then I'd better be very careful what I say to you, hadn't I, sweet, because I am not going to be accused of giving you information that old Andrew might like the pleasure of imparting."

Quite suddenly Lisa was parted from him in a most unexpected way. He had been propelling her towards an old-fashioned lift in the tube station, after they had landed on the Embankment. The lift was crowded. Lisa was already on but the attendant pushed Tobias back, and slammed home the gates.

She was dizzy with relief that she had got away from him without having to make a scene. He would run up the stairs, she supposed, and anyway, he would be there outside her house tomorrow, waiting for her, and giving rise to talk. Already the neighbours were saying pointed things about her handsome boy-friend, and because of his manner, Lisa supposed they could be forgiven for not entirely believing her when she kept insisting that it was only her husband's half-brother.

With the hunted feeling she had acquired in the last day or two, she got on an up train instead of the down train she needed, and she got off two stations further on, and played safe by taking a bus home.

Mrs. Cobb met her at the door. "What happened, dear? *He's* been on the telephone, to know if you were home yet. Rare upset he was."

"Upset?" Lisa found that hard to believe.

"Well, cross, I suppose, as much as anything. Didn't you have a nice day? I didn't know you'd planned to slip off with him. You might have told me what you were doing."

"But I didn't. I didn't plan to meet him. It's so stupid but he gave young Roddy the impression he was my boy-friend and now no-one will believe me.

I can't get rid of him. He's one of Andrew's half-brothers, and from what he tells me, he was more than friendly with Andrew's first wife. But then, how can that be? Andrew wouldn't have him there, would he? And the housekeeper wouldn't make such a pet of him if that were so, would she?"

"If you ask me, dear, you've married into a rather peculiar family. I wouldn't get above myself and advise you, but I can tell you this. If it was me I'd be on the telephone to my husband and I'd tell him his half-brother was being a nuisance, just in case anyone else decided to make it known to him. I don't say they would, mind, but I'd just take care to get in first."

"I don't want to worry him. Still, I was going to telephone Andrew tonight. Perhaps I will tell him, at that, only it's difficult, as I'm not supposed to know about Tobias."

"Seems this Tobias chap made himself known to you, so there was nothing much you could do about it, was there?"

"He's the sort of man who could make someone like me look rather silly if she made a scene over his attentions. He just doesn't go too far, yet he makes me feel he would, if he had half a chance – or worse, he'd make other people think I'd let him go too far, and I think that would amuse him very much."

"Yes, I know what you mean, dear. I've met chaps like him before. Well, you think about it. I shall be in the kitchen, so you'll be able to feel free to talk to your young husband."

Lisa hadn't telephoned Andrew since the first day she had arrived and discovered what Mrs. Cobb's trouble was. She had forced herself not to telephone him, every day, for fear he should think she was being a nuisance. Andrew was so undemonstrative.

She pulled up a chair and was about to pick up the telephone, when it started to ring.

For a moment she wasn't going to answer it, thinking it might be Tobias. When she did answer it, however, it was Andrew.

"How are you, Lisa?" he asked her.

"I'm fine. I didn't want to worry you

by calling you before this," she said. "Are you all right?"

"Yes, pretty well, but my father isn't. He's in bed. I hate to ask you this, Lisa, just when you must be feeling you've settled in again at No. 19, but it would help me a lot if you could come back, if only for a couple of weeks."

"Of course I will, darling," she said. Now, she told herself, in thankfulness, she wouldn't even have to mention the prickly subject of Tobias. Now she could go back without having to admit that she had seen Tobias at the house before she left, and not asked Andrew about him.

Andrew talked quickly, as if one eye was on the clock. "I've still got one or two calls to make. Surgery was overfull tonight," he admitted in the end. "I'll have to go now. When shall I expect you?"

"Tomorrow. I'll get an early train. Or I'll come tonight if you like," she amended, thinking how difficult it would be if Tobias turned up on the doorstep and insisted on accompanying her back to Queensmarket in one of those slow, old fashioned trains.

"Could you?" Andrew surprised her by saying. "Mrs. Tabb's got her hands full, and the District Nurse is pretty busy at the moment, too."

Lisa said, in a stifled voice, "I've missed you, Andrew."

He took his time about answering that, and when he did, it was to say, "Have you?"

Not a terribly satisfying telephone call, but Lisa had little time to think about it if she was to catch that train.

Mrs. Cobb said, "Well, I shall miss you, dear, but I can't help feeling it's for the best. What will I tell that rascal if he turns up bold as brass asking for you?"

"Tell him I told my husband about him," Lisa said, on inspiration. "I didn't, because I didn't have a chance. He's full of his father's illness and being rushed off his feet, and I think I detected a note of wistfulness in his voice when he spoke about London. Oh, wouldn't it be wonderful if we could both come back here together? You'd stay wouldn't you, and look after us?"

"I would, if you're sure that's what you'd want, dear. When couples haven't been married long, there's an awful lot of adjusting to do, and you don't want anyone else around."

"I'd want you, Mrs. Cobb. You understand people so well," Lisa said, with a tremulous smile.

"Well, if that's what you think, then don't be so long coming back next time. There's your taxi at the door. Better get a move on, dear — them clocks are ticking up all the time."

Darkness was falling. The bright street lamps of London made big brilliant blobs in the dusk; white lights in the side roads, and burning orange bars where the giant standards suspended over the main roads. Lisa felt torn in two — wanting London and the suburbs so much, yet aching to return to Andrew's side. Would there be any peace of mind for her?

Her train was in the station. She was lucky enough to find an empty carriage. She settled back in the corner with a sigh. Now she could relax and think about Andrew, and what she would say to him.

She hadn't been in her seat above a minute, before a stout woman puffed along the platform, looked into Lisa's compartment, and got in. There was a puzzled look, a start of half recognition, as though the woman had seen Lisa before, but couldn't remember her name.

Lisa had seen the woman in church. What bad luck that someone from Queensmarket should choose just this compartment to travel in.

Lisa firmly put her magazine up in front of her face, though she was in no mood for reading. And then the train's whistle blew. Footsteps, the inevitable late ones, thudded alongside the train. Lisa prayed that no-one else would get in, in case it was someone from Queensmarket who did realise who she was.

"He'll never make it," the woman muttered, and helpfully threw open the door. Lisa looked up, to find herself staring in dismay up into the face of Tobias.

"Oh, no," she gasped, in sheer despair.

"Did you think I wouldn't make it?" he said joyously, and pulled himself in as the train started. "Trust old Toby – pity we couldn't get a carriage to ourselves, though," and he turned to smile impudently at the stout woman.

She went scarlet. "I've just remembered where I've seen you before," she said to Lisa. "It's Dr. Andrew's new wife isn't it?"

Lisa looked helplessly from her to Tobias. He wasn't in the least put out. "And you," he said to the woman, "are Mrs. Miggle from the corn chandlers' at the back of the Town Hall, and you do the brasses in church. I never forget a face, or a name."

She muttered something and got up. Tobias helpfully gathered her parcels together for her. "Shall I find you a nice corner seat somewhere?" he asked her charmingly.

"No, please don't go, Mrs. Miggle," Lisa pleaded, genuinely wishing the woman would stay. Tobias was the last person she wanted to be alone with.

The woman gave Lisa a reproachful stare. "I've never stayed where I'm not wanted, not in my life, and I don't intend to start now."

13

THE last thing that Lisa had expected was to find Andrew at the station to meet her.

It had been a most uncomfortable journey. She had tried to find a seat in Mrs. Miggle's compartment, but it was full up. The next best thing seemed to stand in the corridor outside, in full view of the woman, so that she shouldn't imagine heaven knew what. There was no doubting that stare of hers, as she went. Her very back bristled with self-righteous indignation.

But of course, nothing that Lisa could do now would alter things because of the way Tobias had looked at Lisa when he had got in the compartment, and the things he had said suggested that this had been a pre-arranged meeting, or at least discussed. And she herself must have looked filled with guilt when she had realised that somehow, whether by design or sheer accident, he had discovered she was travelling on that train.

Tobias vanished as the train steamed into Queensmarket. Lisa didn't see what happened to him. He must have gone on to Skegwell when he saw Andrew on the platform. And now Lisa was in a most unenviable position. If she told Andrew about Tobias being on the train, he would want to know why she hadn't said anything about Tobias on the telephone earlier. And if she didn't say anything about Tobias being on the train, what would Andrew think if that tiresome Mrs. Miggle started talking?

As Andrew seemed so touchingly pleased to see her, it seemed a pity to spoil it by mentioning Tobias at all. She made a snap decision and didn't tell him.

"Lisa, darling, did you have a good journey?" he began.

"Fair. It's not a bad train. I'm so glad to be back," she could say with truth. "I was mad keen to get away, and then I wanted to be back."

"No-one is more glad than I, to hear you say that," Andrew told her, as he edged her through the crush at the barrier, and out to where his car stood in the station yard. "I know it's only a short walk, but I called for your train on the way home. I've been at Shapplegate farm again. It's been quite a week. Tell me about you. What did you find to do with yourself?"

"I took a small boy to the Zoo one day and got worn out," she said carefully. That made Andrew laugh.

"And I established very comfortable relations with Mrs. Cobb, who has agreed to stay on indefinitely and look after me when I go back to London. I got most of my old pupils back, though I told them it was only for a month. Mrs. Cobb said she'd explain that my father-in-law was ill. How ill is he, Andrew?"

"Bad enough, and I was rather hoping you'd help me in surgery, Lisa. You just wear a white coat and hold babies for me and children who won't keep still. That sort of thing, oh, and writing up the cards. Do you think you could? It would help such a lot. I'm afraid being single-handed and working round the clock is getting me down."

"Of course, Andrew, I'd love to. That

was my main grouch when I was here before – no-one would let me help them."

"And it would help Mrs. Tabb if you'd take the telephone calls and answer the door, now my father's ill. Would you? I know it will curtail your freedom in the mornings and evenings, but you can go out in the afternoons if you want to. Your friend Hazel has missed you, she tells me."

And that was all the conversation they had before driving into the familiar square. The door of The Old House stood open, and Lisa fancied it was a welcome for her, until common sense told her it was to save Mrs. Tabb from having to let them in, Andrew always mislaying his keys.

"Shall I look at your father and say hallo?" Lisa proposed, at the foot of the stairs, after Mrs. Tabb had ceremoniously come out of the kitchen to greet her and to vanish almost at once.

"I don't think I should. I've given him something to make him sleep," Andrew said quickly.

"All right," Lisa said, quietly. She went

upstairs. Nothing had changed really. Her father-in-law didn't want to see her, no matter how Andrew tried to cover up, and Mrs. Tabb liked her no more than at first. So long as she could call her Miss Lisa and treat her like a child, she was all right, but now that a job had been given to Lisa, so that she could be treated as a responsible human being, Mrs. Tabb didn't like it. That was plain, Lisa fretted.

She went naturally into the big room where she had slept with Andrew that night. But it was shut and she couldn't get the door open.

"Lisa, I forgot," Andrew said, pelting up the stairs behind her. "Mrs. Tabb persuaded the decorators to come in while you were away, so we're back in the other room. It won't be long before the big room is ready. It will look rather nice."

She nodded. She wanted to cry out, "Are we sleeping together in my bed?" but she dare not. Andrew was suddenly unapproachable again, and the hostile air of the house was enveloping her. She was tired. She wanted something to eat, but Mrs. Tabb hadn't suggested food, and gave the impression that she was run off her feet, so Lisa decided to say nothing, and to prepare for bed.

The familiar cold of the atmosphere was immediately noticeable. She opened the window and stood listening to Andrew's footsteps going down the stairs, and the telephone ringing. He would be going out, she knew, out into that moaning wind. He wouldn't mind, not really. This was his home town. He liked it, understood it. It had been stupid wishful thinking on her part to expect him to want to go back to No. 19 with her.

The sea was coming in, with a crash and a strong hissing as it retreated. How she hated the sound of it. And there was the restless flicking of the beam from the lighthouse, across the night sky, like a mischievous child playing with a torch. She would never sleep tonight, she knew.

And then Mrs. Tabb knocked on the door and came in. She was carrying a tray. "Dr. Andrew said you looked peaky and tired so I thought you might like to get into bed and have this. Don't be long getting undressed because it's good hot soup and the sandwiches are fresh. Local-killed chicken, none of your frozen packaged stuff you get in London."

"Oh, Mrs. Tabb, how good of you. You shouldn't have dragged up here for my sake. I'd have come down."

"I don't drag anywhere, miss – I'm as spry as you are, though I am twice or three times your age. And who said you were wanted downstairs, anyway?"

Lisa flushed, deeply hurt. "I'm sorry, I only thought – " She broke off suddenly as a thought occurred to her, and before she could stop herself, his name had popped out. "Tobias – he's downstairs."

Mrs. Tabb's face confirmed that that was true. So he had come back after all, and only Mrs. Tabb knew that he had been in London with Lisa because she had told him Lisa's address. Before Lisa could point this out, Mrs. Tabb got in first.

"So it's true what he says – you did know him first. And that's why you were so anxious to go to London, hoping he'd follow you. Now we know why you were always coming in late for meals, and never able to say where you'd been. Pretending to be so innocent."

"That's not true, not any of it. I didn't even know him before. I just saw him that day — he spoke to me in a Bar — "

"In a Bar? So you go to those places, do you? What would my poor Andrew say if he knew — he thinks you're such a child."

"I don't go to those places. I just went that day because — "

Again Lisa broke off. How could she admit to Mrs. Tabb that she had heard the late Tressida Lee frequented that Bar because she had accidentally discovered the very beauty parlour that Tressida had used. How could she say in so many words to Mrs. Tabb that she had an over-riding desire to know what Tressida had been like, what she did, where she went? But she couldn't let Mrs. Tabb accuse her of frequenting bars so she said indignantly: "I was just curious to know what it was like."

Mrs. Tabb smiled pityingly. "Oh, I suppose you've been asking questions about Dr. Andrew's first wife. She did things that you would do better not to try to do, miss, if you don't want to break his heart. People forgave her – she could get away with anything, because she was so beautiful, and she had such an air. She wound people round her little finger and they loved it. You couldn't do the things she did, and don't you dare try."

"Why are you being like this to me, Mrs. Tabb? You weren't like it that first day that Andrew brought me home here? Why? What went wrong?"

"Nothing went wrong. Nothing has changed, except that I could do nothing else but to be pleasant to you that first day. How could I hurt him by being otherwise? And don't think I've singled you out to be anything special. I haven't. You couldn't rate for any special treatment, good or bad, but even if you could, it's not the point. It's not just you I didn't want here – it's any wife of his. I didn't want Dr. Andrew to marry anyone else, not again. He's had one marriage. He deserves some peace, not to go through a second marriage that could never be like the first."

Lisa sat down limply on the bed and

stared at the cooling food. Her appetite had gone.

Her heart pumped frantically, when she thought of Tobias downstairs, telling Mrs. Tabb lies about her. What chance did she stand?

She wondered if Andrew realised that his half-brother had followed Lisa to London, or whether only Mrs. Tabb knew. Why had Mrs. Tabb told Tobias the address, so that he could go to London after her? Was Mrs. Tabb trying to break up a new marriage she didn't approve off? Or was she another of these people who worshipped the memory of the late Tressida Lee, and couldn't bear to see someone else step into her shoes?

She was asleep when Andrew came up to bed, so again he went into the dressing-room. He had had a session with Mrs. Tabb, and he wanted to ask Lisa for the truth.

He couldn't believe it. He knew, of course, that there was 'feeling' on Mrs. Tabb's part. She had been shocked to hear of his marrying again. He had expected that. Mrs. Tabb had been in the house since girlhood. She looked on herself as part of the family. She worshipped his father and had adored the first bride to be brought to The Old House. In an unhappy place, Tressida had shone like a bright jewel.

But for Mrs. Tabb to have said those things about Lisa, had cut him to the heart. If they were untrue, then Mrs. Tabb must go, and that would make a great deal of trouble with his father. But what if those things hadn't been untrue?

He stood looking down at Lisa, whose tears had long since dried and sleep had claimed her. She slept with the exquisite careless abandon of a young child; her long dark lashes lay fanning her cheeks, those cheeks which were so white and smooth. Her mouth, innocent of make-up, was darkly pink and beautifully modelled, sweet in repose, with no guile, no tension. There was no tension in any part of that face, nor of that body. Relaxed, peaceful, Lisa lay dreaming that she had Andrew back and that the shadows had receded; her enemies had gone and even the lighthouse had vanished. She was back with Andrew and Mrs. Cobb, safe in that quiet suburb of London, with her own roof above her. Her peace of mind reflected itself all over her, and Andrew, pushing one finger through the loosely hanging fingers of her right hand, halfway over the edge of the bed, found it terribly difficult to believe that Lisa had been in London with Tobias.

He would have to take it up with her, of course. He shrank from it. If it weren't true, she would know that he had doubted her. If it were true, what on earth was he going to say to her?

He bent and kissed her forehead, and took his things into the dressing-room with him, quietly closing the door. But he hadn't been asleep long before the telephone rang and he was called out.

He came back at five, and overslept, and had to start surgery without any breakfast. Mrs. Tabb was cross at the good food being spoiled, going to waste. His father was inclined to be fractious. Tobias was tiresome.

"Look," Andrew said, with rare anger, "you may have been welcome in this house before my return, but you are not welcome any longer."

Tobias looked taken aback. "Oh, I say,

dear boy," he drawled, "what's wrong? You never minded one way or the other, and frankly I can't think what you'll get out of being unpleasant to me. Until the old man tells me to clear out, then I stay as long as it suits me."

"No. Not any more. The old man is ill and dependent on me. I go, if you stay. It's as simple as that. I think you'll find which one of us he prefers, but take it from me, there isn't room for both of us."

As he said it, his ears were straining for a sound of Lisa coming down. She had still been sleeping, and in spite of his telling her he wanted her in surgery with him this morning, Andrew had let her sleep after all. She didn't look really well; not exactly unwell, but rather frail. It was difficult to put a finger on it, but it had stayed his hand when he had been about to grasp her shoulder and wake her.

Tobias had no such scruples. He would cheerfully have dragged Lisa into this. He did his best.

"It's the young innocent been mixing things, is it?" he said, with a twisted smile. “Dear old Andrew Head-in-the-Clouds, wake up. Wake up about that little new wife of yours. She’ll have you in the dog-house in no time at all.”

The clump of shoes in the waiting-room reminded them that the patients were arriving. They lowered their voices, but Mrs. Tabb in the kitchen knew that it was not from delicacy but from anger. They would both flare out any minute, and how was she going to keep the early arrivals out there from hearing?

“Just what do you mean by that?” she heard Andrew grit out to Tobias.

Tobias shrugged. “You wouldn’t believe we had a thumping good time together in London, but this might help to convince you,” and he took from his pocket an orange folder, the type containing negatives and fresh-developed prints.

“Go on, look at them. She makes a pretty picture, and in case you’re tempted to do them a mischief, let me remind you that they don’t belong to you.”

Andrew got them out and looked at them – eight prints of the Zoo background, Lisa alone in them. In the print on the top, she had turned a radiant face to the camera, evidently surprised at being caught unaware of the person taking the pictures.

It was young Roddy's camera. The background was slightly askew. That should have told Andrew that Tobias would have been unlikely to have made that error. But Andrew was too angry to notice such fine points. He only had eyes for Lisa's happy face, and Tobias's assertion that he had been behind the camera at the time.

"You stay on here, old boy," Tobias said pleasantly. "You curry favour with the old man, but every time you look at Lisa, remember the London Zoo, oh, and the Tower, and the water-bus, and the lift – such a lot of memories we have to share, Lisa and I. 'Bye for now."

Having done his best, Tobias went. Andrew heard him saying goodbye to Mrs. Tabb. "Kicked out by old Andrew. What about that?" Andrew heard him say.

And then Lisa came downstairs.

"Oh, Andrew, I'm so sorry. I overslept. Shouldn't you be in surgery? It's time, isn't it?"

His angry face startled her. "I am aware of the time," he said shortly. He had never spoken to her quite like that before.

"What's the matter, Andrew?" she gasped.

"There isn't time to tell you. As you've just pointed out to me, there isn't time. What's wrong with you, Lisa, you look terrible," he said, in a changed voice, concern replacing his former bitter tone.

"I've only just woken up and I've got a headache," she said. She, too, was now unwilling to discuss something pleasantly. She guessed Mrs. Tabb had said something to Andrew; probably the loathsome Tobias, also. "Do you want me to come and help you?" she added.

"No, thanks, go out and get some fresh air or something." If he had her in surgery with him, it would be on his mind and he would feel impelled to say something. There wouldn't be time to thrash it out between patients, and to half discuss a subject as important as this, and leave it in the air, would be disastrous.

So he battled through surgery that

morning on his own. Lisa, in the sitting-room, heard a baby screaming and longed to go in and lend a hand, but dare not. Later, a small boy bellowed in fear, and kept stampeding to the door, his mother more hindrance than help, to judge by the things she was shouting at Andrew, but again Lisa dared not intrude for fear of making things worse.

When she could bear it no longer, she got up and knocked on old Dr. Lee's door and asked if she could go in and visit him.

Receiving a grunt from within, she opened the door.

He was sitting up in bed reading the newspapers. He took off his glasses with exaggerated care and waited till she had said what she had to. She felt so unwanted, in the way, that she almost backed out at once.

"Well, come in, girl, don't stand there letting a draught in."

She shut the door carefully after her and came round the bed to stand by him.

"What is it? Has the cat got your tongue?"

"It's no good you going on at me like that," she said quietly. "It won't do you any good, because it doesn't really matter any more."

"What's that? What's that?"

"You've made it plain that you don't like me. So has Mrs. Tabb. And now Andrew is looking at me as if he wished I just wasn't here."

"Well, if you think that, why come back?" Dr. Lee growled.

"Because of your illness. Andrew asked me to come back and help him – last night. Now he seems to have changed his mind. It's the influence of this place, constantly reminding him of his first wife. I'm positive of that. So I'm going to ask him to go back to London with me. If he won't go, then I'm going. Out of his life. Because if I stay here it will get worse and worse. I know that, in my heart."

He stared up at her for a long time. At last, he said, "Why did you marry my son?"

It wasn't what she had expected, but she answered firmly enough: "Every woman wants to marry. I suppose he was the one person I felt I would want to be married to."

"I thought you were going to declare that you loved him. Thanks for sparing me that."

"It doesn't concern you, Dr. Lee, what my private feelings are," she said with dignity. "You've had a large hand in making me feel an outsider. You've taken your son away from me before I had a chance to prove that I might be just as good for him as his first wife."

He put his book down then, and his spectacles on top. "What makes you think you are qualified to even mention *her*?"

"Qualified?" Lisa retorted. "I'll tell you why I'm qualified. Because I've been subjected to comparisons with her ever since I came here. Mrs. Tabb took against me on sight, though she pretended she didn't. And everyone who knew that other girl, has said something or other about her to make me perpetually aware that even though she's dead, her ghost is still going to dog my footsteps. If only I could see a picture of her, hear a record of her voice, so that I could know what I was up against, but I get such a muddled picture of her from other people. I just wish I had never heard of her," Lisa finished passionately.

"Who has talked about her and what did they say?"

She looked suspiciously at him. He didn't usually encourage her talk.

"Come on, girl, where's your tongue. And don't stand over me. Never could bear that. Fetch a chair."

She did as he asked. "From Mrs. Tabb I learned that she was tall, and that she could get away with anything, she was so charming. From the organist I learned that she was beautiful, but he – well, he didn't seem to get on with her."

Dr. Lee grunted. "That young fool. I'd like to know what he knew about her, to feel qualified to judge."

"You did ask me. Everyone seems to remember her as such an outstanding person, with me a very pale also-ran. If I'd known what Andrew's first wife was remembered as, I don't think I'd have come here in the first place."

"And if you'd never come here in the first place? If you'd managed to keep my son away from here, what then? What sort of life had you in mind for him?" Dr. Lee asked, not sourly now, but as if he really wanted to know.

"The sort of life you dragged us from. We had our own roof over our heads – "

"Yours – not his. This is his roof."

"No. Dr. Lee, this is yours; yours and Mrs. Tabb's. I shall never be welcome here. I can see that. A woman wants her own place, to make it into a home in her own way. I wanted to do just that. To cook and wash and sew for him, to help him enjoy his leisure, and to bring up his children, God willing."

He looked sharply at her. "Children are a mixed blessing," he said shortly. "Everyone who hasn't got them, wants them, and when they come, there's the usual yearning for the times when the children weren't there, and there was leisure and more money."

"Don't worry, I'm not likely to have a family."

"What makes you say that?" he asked her.

"Because Andrew doesn't seem to want a family. He says I'm only a child myself, which is as nice a way of getting out of parenthood as any, I suppose. I can't imagine children in this cold miserable house, anyway."

"Don't blame or criticise where you don't know your facts," he told her wearily. "I had the same ideas, long ago. I loved a woman. Love! That's an over-rated element if there ever was one. My best friend took her from me. But still I was fool enough to want a family. There have always been Lees in this house. I wanted to carry on the tradition. Sons to be doctors, like me." His mouth turned down. "The woman I married gave me Tobias, whom I believe you know." He glared at her. "And Quentin, whom I trust you don't know."

"I've heard about him, from Tobias," she told him coolly.

"Um. Well, I still wasn't cured of hankering for a family. When she died, I married again. I know all about second-best. I didn't want that for my son Andrew. He was all I wished for in a son. A good lad. A good medical man. Had to be persuaded to be a G.P. but he does his duty. I was determined he should have the woman he loved, and I tried to save him from second-best. But no-one takes any notice of older folk."

"What's so special about age, that makes you think you know everything about everyone else?" she cried.

"Experience comes with age," he said flatly. "Oh, I know it isn't everyone who can profit by experience. But I fancy I have done as well with the experience flung into my path, as any man. A G.P. sees the seedy side of life. He knows, I suppose, most of the answers if not all of them."

"Other people have said something similar about you," Lisa admitted. "Hazel Edwards. She said a good G.P. is almost as good as a cleric, and you are a good G.P. she says."

"Bully for her," he said sourly. "Well, you've got your answer. And I still maintain that I know best where my son Andrew is concerned."

"You go right ahead believing that," Lisa said, in a low tone. "And when you've lost him altogether, as I believe you will, don't blame me. Be fair and admit that you've driven him away. I shall do my best to stop you, because he loves you and he needs you as much as he needs me. And don't you forget that I came here prepared to try and make everyone like me, and I also came hoping to find a father. I haven't got one. I haven't got anyone except Andrew, and I badly wanted a family. You just remember that, Dr. Lee."

He raised his bushy eyebrows at her. "I can be fair. If you make my son Andrew happy, if you convince me you're the right one for him, I'll take back everything I've said. *If* you do."

"That's it, isn't it? Who's the judge? You'll swear I haven't, and you'll probably take a hand in making sure I can't make Andrew happy. By the way, what did his first wife call you?"

Real pain flared in his face. She was startled. "I only asked because I've been warned by Mrs. Tabb not to dare trespass and use the same name to you, but if I don't know what it was, how can I know I'm doing the wrong thing?" Lisa reasoned.

"You don't call me anything but Dr. Lee," he pointed out.

"And it seems likely that I shall go on

calling you that, if you keep me at arm's length," she said bitterly. "All right, don't tell me if you don't want me to know. I'm not surprised."

He let her go. He lay back exhausted listening to her light feet tap-tapping through the hall to the outer vestibule. She had grabbed her overcoat on the way out, and was shrugging it on, to huddle into against the wind, as she went down the path. He would have given a lot to undo that interview with her, take back every word he had said, and start all over again. But what else would he have said, to take the place of the words they had hurled at each other? She had come into the room to do battle with him. But, he had to admit in all fairness, it had not been of her making. She was retaliating, protecting her own: her little niche she had carved in a lonely world, her chance of happiness and her opportunity to give of herself.

He wondered where she was going. Lisa herself had no idea. She threshed her way against the wind, through the square, blindly towards Hazel and the vicarage.

Zillie Denner looked out of his shop door. "Lisa – it is good to see you. Come in, come in, my young friend," he called.

It was as good a refuge as anywhere. "Hello," she said and took his outstretched hands.

"You were coming to see me, perhaps?" he suggested.

"Honestly, I hadn't much idea where I was going. I've just had a row with my father-in-law."

"Ah, that man." Zillie was disgusted. "He is his own worst enemy. Many is the time I have told him so. I tell you, child, when the east wind cuts at my old chest and I am forced to go and consult him, we have what you call *words*. He is a fine doctor but a child when it is time to control his temper which he does not do. What did you quarrel with him about?"

"Oh, it doesn't matter," she said, wishing she hadn't spoken like that of Dr. Lee. "Anyway, who would believe me? Not him. Not even my dear Andrew, I daresay, when they get at him."

"Ah, now, that is another matter. (Cocoa? I thought I might have to make a double helping. It was a little bird whispered). I have to do something which may make you angry with me. I trust you will remember that I speak as a friend. I have to tell you of rumour and to ask that you say something to me about it." He was being so earnest that his almost perfect English deserted him this morning and he strung all his words together in a very un-English way.

"I'll try," Lisa said.

"There is a woman who is in the cornchandlers' called Mrs. Miggle. This Mrs. Miggle gossips. She gossips of you."

"Oh, not already? Oh, dear, now what am I going to do?" Lisa cried in despair. "And you want to know my side of it? The trouble is that the most charitable person breathing would have been forgiven for getting the wrong impression," and very briefly she told Zillie about the Zoo day, the day on the water-bus and the train journey home, and exactly how much Tobias figured in those trips.

"I suppose I must have looked as if I knew him very well and had been seeing him recently — I remember I was dismayed, angry, helpless, because I couldn't get free of him. He's an awful person. The more I kept telling him to leave me alone, the more he insisted that I didn't mean it and that I really liked him. What can one do with such a person?"

"Oy-oy-*oy*," Zillie muttered. "It is difficult. But then, *Tobias*." He shrugged.

"Would you say he was worse than his brother?"

"His brother Quentin? Ah, now, there was a bad hat. He was a confidence man, so they say. It never came to trial because he escaped in a plane, which came down. A blessing in disguise, because it was only himself and the pilot and this little plane, which fell into the North Sea and the pilot was afterwards rescued. But it saved the doctor and his family from much legal trouble and publicity."

"What does Tobias do for a living?" Lisa asked.

"Nothing. He is no good. His father sends him money. He has some money which he inherited from his mother. Ah, but he is no good, that one. Women — oy-oy-oy."

"Yes, don't I know it? Zillie, please be a good friend and tell me some things I want to know," Lisa pleaded. "You see, it's hard to explain, but I feel that the shadow of the first Mrs. Lee is so black over me that it isn't only pushing me out of this place, but it's pushing me out of Andrew's life. If I could only know what I'm up against."

"You have asked me this before. What is it you want me to tell you?"

"Well, if she was alive today and came walking down the square – tell me what you would see."

"But how would it help you?" he wanted to know. "I should see her as a man sees as woman."

"That's it. That's exactly what I want to hear."

"But Lisa *liebchen*, this is very embarrassing," he protested.

"*Please*, Zillie."

"Well," he spluttered, "well, now, she was beautiful. Very, very beautiful."

"That's what everyone says. But *how*?"

"I am not much good at describing people," he excused himself.

"Try," she urged.

"Well, let us say that if I were a young man, I would neglect my work for thinking about her, and I would not be able to sleep at nights, for remembering the way she talked, and when she used to come into my shop and plead with me for that piano – ach, the way she pleaded, I wonder I did not give it to her – and her voice was so soft and like velvet, and her eyes promised things – but what am I saying? She was Dr. Andrew's wife. Go away, *liebchen*, or I shall be telling things I have no wish to even remember."

She sighed. "This is what I get from everyone. Why did Andrew marry me then?"

"Do you not *know*? And you, his wife?" Zillie was shocked. "But that is another matter?"

She left him with the feeling that he had failed her, and that he might well see her leaving Queensmarket in a hurry again, and this time for good.

From Zillie's shop Lisa drifted to the vicarage. Hazel was making up lists with the aid of her father's diary. She was only too glad of an excuse to put the job away and make some tea.

"I've missed you, Lisa," she said, but she frowned as she said it. "I suppose I ought to wait for you to tell me what was really behind that hurried departure of yours, but I ought to warn you that there's a lot of talk flying around."

"Mrs. Miggle," Lisa said. "I know. Zillie's just told me. I suppose I can't do better than to give you my side of it just as I gave it to him, only I can give you a lot more frilly details of what Tobias said and did and the way he looked at me while he was saying and doing those things. I hate him."

Hazel sat still and listened. Her very stillness and patience in listening warned Lisa of how serious all this was, because normally Hazel wasn't a very still sort of person and she rarely waited for Lisa to stop talking before she butted in. They usually both joyously talked at the same time and managed to keep up with what the other person was saying.

"The thing is, has Andrew heard any of this, and what on earth shall I do now?" Lisa fretted.

"I think you're all right, Lisa, because so many people like you here although they don't know you very well. But the thing is, we all know Tobias. It's history repeating itself."

"How do you mean?" Lisa asked slowly.

"Well, you know about the accident – Tobias knocking Mollie Kidman down on the crossing. It was Tressida Lee who was with him at the time, and everyone says that there was a lot of hushing up done there. No-one really knows the half of it. I'm not saying she was unfaithful to Andrew – I don't believe she could be unfaithful to anyone. Not that she was so good – oh, I'm not telling this very well. What I mean is, Tressida would have regarded being unfaithful as very risky and foolish, and she never did anything that was risky or foolish." She stared at Lisa's astonished face.

"You know, I don't think I would have liked Tressida Lee, in spite of everyone saying she was so charming," Lisa said slowly. "I think she sounds as if she might have been a rather selfish type."

But Hazel, who was usually so blunt and outspoken, had nothing to say about that.

"Oh, well, if I go from here suddenly,

it'll be because I just can't stand it," Lisa said unhappily. "I was so glad when Andrew asked me to come back. I thought he missed me. Then it all changed once we were in the house and Mrs. Tabb was there and old Dr. Lee was being doped and couldn't be seen and, oh, I don't know. I just felt like a stranger in the place on sufferance."

Hazel bit her lip and said nothing.

"How's Nigel?" Lisa asked, changing the subject.

Hazel's face lit. "You'll be glad to hear we've buried the hatchet and we might, with a push from some helpful person, be persuaded to go steady."

"Oh, Hazel, I'm so glad. Really I am. He's so nice," Lisa exclaimed. "Do keep it going. Don't be tempted to argue or fight with him and lose ground. I'd like to see you two happy together."

"Any message for him next time I go?" Hazel twinkled.

"Yes, tell him not to go near the lighthouse again."

Hazel's jaw dropped. "What do *you* know about the lighthouse?"

"Well, I asked him what happened to

him and he started to tell me about how he went there about an extra for the choir, and that he fell down the steps, then he wouldn't say any more. So my message to him is that if he's not careful of stone steps he shouldn't go near the lighthouse."

"Oh, I though for one awful moment that he told you how he came to fall," Hazel said. "Well, come to think of it, I don't mind you knowing. You see, I was there, too. We'd been arguing. Gosh, how we do argue. I suppose we were both a bit edgy because at that time if anyone'd said he was going to be the man I'd think of marrying, I would have laughed at them, because I couldn't stand him. Biological chemical reaction or whatever it's called. I didn't think he might be the same."

"Go on," Lisa begged. It was oddly comforting to know that other people had their ups and downs and that it had turned out all right.

"That's about it. We were on edge, ready to flare up at any minute and he left something behind and I made a pointed remark about having to go all the way to the top and he turned sharply, to make a witty come-back, I suppose, and he missed his footing and fell. I suppose it was my fault, though I was more furious than anything else because even after he got taken to hospital we had our differences." She grinned. "Me being me and him being him, we'll never run smooth, I expect. He's one of those awful clots who never knows when they're letting secrets out, and that I cannot stand. And that is only one thing about him that I still don't like."

"But you are in love with him, aren't you?"

"If by that you mean am I on the point of agreeing to marry him because I feel guilty about his accident, well, you know me. Am I likely to do such a daft thing? I'd say the accident was as much his fault as mine, on sober reflection, and that I suppose I must be in love with him to take him on for life anyway. And I'm doing it with my eyes wide open. Some people want their heads examined."

Lisa felt much better for her talk with Hazel, than she had with her session with Zillie. Hazel was so refreshing, she dwarfed all one's worries in the process of telling of her own.

It was still too early to go back for lunch, and having left the house, Lisa wasn't going to risk bringing Mrs. Tabb to the front door just to ask if she would be wanted for taking phone calls. Andrew might have felt like enlisting her aid last night but it was doubtful if he would want to see her around today, until he was ready to have that threatened talk with her.

Lisa remembered the invitation to Carmichael Mawson's farm and, after consulting the bus times, she managed to catch one almost at once. The crossroads he had mentioned weren't far away and she got off the bus with a lot of time to kill.

There was a telephone box at the corner. She called up the farm to see if it was all right to go there before lunch. She had the feeling now, that she wouldn't be in the district long and that she wanted to get this visit over and make sure of it.

Carmichael answered, "Lisa? Is anything wrong?" he asked.

"Yes. I might be leaving Queensmarket

soon. I would like to see you and I've got a chance this morning, but if it's going to put you out, then I'll try and manage tomorrow."

"I just happened to be in the house and heard the telephone but actually I've got to go over to Horrocks – well, you won't know him, but it's a good three miles but I should be back in time for lunch. You'll stay and eat with us, won't you? Meanwhile I'm sure my Mrs. Reckless would love to have you."

Lisa said she would like to spend some time with Mrs. Reckless and that she hadn't forgotten the harmonium.

She walked up the long rutted road to the footpath he had told her about, and then she saw Elmgates.

It was a long, low building of local stone with an attractively humped roof. Masses of trees banked behind one end of the property, barns and outhouses with thatched roofs at the other end. There really were elms, too, with rooks' nests in them, and the elms were near the big gates. Lisa liked that.

Nearer the farmhouse the place was kept up very well. The drive was well weeded and reasonably free from ruts. The grass was kept short and tidy in front of the farmhouse and there were a few rosebeds, but mostly herbs. A wistaria grew thickly over a trellis porch and a five-fingered creeper clung precariously to the brick wall of the verandah at one end. A jasmine found a foothold on the wooden wall of a summerhouse in the front garden. Wherever possible there was a flowering climbing plant. At one time this must have been a very well-kept and beautiful place, but it was clear for anyone to see — the money had all gone. Carmichael was what was called 'comfortably off' but no longer rich.

Mrs. Reckless was a mild-looking woman in her late fifties, with plenty of dark hair in a bun on top, dark hair that she later confided to Lisa was kept that nice brown shade by the liberal application at bedtime of good strong cold tea. Mrs. Reckless had made a seed cake that morning and left it to cool on a high window-ledge. She took Lisa into her sitting-room to have a nice cup of tea and a wedge of seed cake to fill a gap, as she explained, until dinner time.

Mrs. Reckless was one of the old brigade who still called the mid-day meal dinner, and the evening meal supper.

She took Lisa past a series of open doors from which a strong smell of beeswax emanated. "It's polishing day," she explained, "and there's a mort of old oak and walnut to be kept shining bright or else that little old woodworm 'll be in it sure as sure."

In the big farm sitting-room there was a low ceiling and Lisa caught a glimpse of twisted chair legs and tall-boys with brass handles, books and willow-pattern china on high shelves, hand blocked linen curtains and covers. A room where strong sunshine shot mote-filled beams across a red tiled floor bright with hand-made rag rugs.

There was a big office with a huge circular table and a tremendous desk near the window, and a pleasant litter of papers that somehow went well with the picture Lisa had of Carmichael.

The farm dining-room was a long bare room with polished floorboards, Queen Anne chairs, an imposing set of silver candelabra on the big side-board with its pot-bellied drawers; a gracious oval table in which the bowl of fruit cast its one reflection as if made of mirror.

"Charming," Lisa breathed.

"I do it all myself, dear. None of these girls from the village for me. Lazy scamps. I used to say to my dear Siddy, never trust to others what you can do yourself, dear. But Siddy, she was too beautiful to soil those hands of hers with housework. Ah, I wish she was here now," she sighed. "But what am I saying, and to you, too."

Lisa took it that it was a relative of the housekeeper, so she smiled vaguely and continued after her.

"You'd like to see a picture of her, though, no doubt? I came across one the other day. I knew there had to be one somewhere and I didn't tell the master, he's so set on no pictures anywhere. I daresay you noticed there was not a frame to be seen. Heathen I call it. A house is not the same without a few pictures about."

"That's what's wrong with The Old House," Lisa said suddenly. "That's what I couldn't make out. I've been wondering why it seems so cold and unfriendly. That's it – no pictures anywhere."

"Ah, yes, they got the notion, too, to do away with pictures, I daresay," Mrs. Reckless said, and looked bothered.

"Is it a new fashion in this part of the world?" Lisa asked.

"Oh, I dare say you could call it that," Mrs. Reckless said, leading the way up three short steps into a long room at the back; a room with half of it railed off as a platform and which would have been quite charming if it hadn't been so madly cluttered.

"This is my little place, my home," Mrs. Reckless said with quiet pride. "And – come on in, dear – this is the picture I mentioned. This is my dear Siddy."

She said it in a hushed voice of quiet pride, worshipful almost. Lisa looked up at the picture, hung above the mantelpiece in solitary state, and she gasped. It took her breath away.

Here was beauty. The face looked straight out of the picture, giving that curious effect of the eyes following the person studying it, but those eyes were green. Whether it was a trick of the photographer's art or whether it was natural, the colour green was startling and lovely, a splendid and perfect foil for the rich copper colour of the quantities of glorious hair. That hair had been dressed in a professional salon; it was pleated and coifed, with one strand of wavy hair finishing in a thick coquettish curl on one shoulder. But it was in keeping.

In keeping with the picture gown, low cut with one strap, of a dull greyish green watered silk. In keeping with the milky white skin and the rather full lips which just escaped being sensuous because of the sweet, rather mischievous smile that curved them. It was in keeping, too, with the fine features, the good bone structure, the small ears, the winged eyebrows. This girl had superb self-confidence, yet there was an abundance of friendliness, the quality perhaps of being able to bring people out, as the saying went. This was undeniable charm, hard to resist, Lisa thought. A person who would dominate any gathering without even trying to.

"She was as clever as she was beautiful," Mrs. Reckless said. "She could do anything, any mortal thing she set her mind to. There was no-one to touch her at anything, and then she had to go and throw herself away on . . . Oh, well, who am I to talk against her? She wanted him. He was the one she had a mind to marry, but she could have had anyone. She could have married a prince."

"Was she your . . . niece, perhaps?" Lisa asked uncertainly.

"My niece? The dear hark at her, the way she talks," Mrs. Reckless appealed to the ceiling. "No, love, she was the master's sister."

The last few words were halting, half whispered, as suddenly the door was banged open and Carmichael stood there, red and angry in the face. He was glaring across at the picture.

"Mrs. Reckless, where did you find that thing? Haven't I told you I want no pictures about the house – *anywhere*?"

"I didn't think you'd mind it in my room, Mr. Carmichael, dear," Mrs. Reckless faltered, and to Lisa's astonishment, she saw tears trickling down the woman's face. "I only brought Miss Lisa in to my room for a cup of tea and some of my nice fresh seedy cake and I thought she'd like to see what Miss Siddy looked like, she was so beautiful."

"Put it back in the attic, Mrs. Reckless," Carmichael said. He had lowered his voice, but he was still very angry. "I'm sorry, Lisa. It's unpardonable of us to let this sort of thing happen the very day you come here. Do forgive me. I wouldn't have had it happen for world."

"But Carmichael, it doesn't matter," Lisa demurred. "Someone who was visiting the hospital when I went there to see the organist, told me about the trouble your family had had with the only girl, so I thought this must be her."

"So people still talk about us. Did you get the full story or only a garbled half?" he retorted grimly.

"I didn't get the whole story because she saw her bus coming," Lisa admitted.

"These damned gossips. Well, you'd better hear the whole of it. She was my sister and we all loved her – everyone did – but she was no good."

"No, sir, don't say that," Mrs. Reckless moaned. "She wasn't bad, not my dear Siddy. No, no, she wasn't bad."

"Don't split hairs. All right, she wasn't personally bad, but she left a trail of havoc behind her. She spoilt everything she touched. And she didn't care. Word it how you like, but that was Tressida's nature. She ruined everything and she didn't *care*."

"*Tressida*?" The name was torn from Lisa.

"Yes. Tressida. Siddy to her family," Carmichael said, his face etched with unhappy lines and his eyes hard. "You wanted to know what she was like, Lisa. Well, now you know."

14

LISA'S legs gave way and she sat down suddenly.

"I didn't know. I didn't know that Andrew's first wife was your sister."

"I'm sorry if it gave you a shock. I thought you must surely know or you wouldn't have hammered at me that night to tell you what she was like. I thought you must surely guess the reason why I wouldn't come in."

"No. And I don't see why you didn't, even now. She's dead. Andrew's still friends with you, isn't he?"

Carmichael and the housekeeper exchanged glances. "Look," he said at last, "I think you'd better leave all this alone, Lisa. If Andrew isn't willing to tell you, I don't think it's my place to. Let it all go, my dear. Be happy with Andrew."

"But I can't – don't you see?" Lisa cried. "I was prepared to try, even when we came here. But every look I got, every word from people, all kept tilting back at that woman who was his first wife."

She looked wildly at the picture. "Everyone gave her such a build-up, so that it made me feel that I had no part in all this. I *had* to find out just what she was like. I just had to. If it had been an ordinary small family in London, where nothing mattered, and they weren't known, it wouldn't have been quite so bad. But here in Queensmarket, the Lees are important. Everyone knew them. And everywhere I went, they knew me, and knew what had gone before, and I didn't. In sheer self-protection, I had to make the effort to find out. But no-one would give me the complete picture."

"I'm sorry, Lisa. You ought never to have come back here with Andrew. But I can see his father's point of view. He wanted a son to carry on the practice. He'd carried on the tradition, and although everyone is fond of saying that the G.P. isn't what he used to be, with the Lees it's different. Old Dr. Lee is the family friend of everyone, and Andrew is, too. Everyone loves them because they are what they are. It would be a pity to break that tradition."

"Well, it's going to be broken all right, isn't it?" she said savagely. "No-one wants children at The Old House, so how can the tradition follow, after Andrew? And if that's the case and it's going to be broken, why can't it be broken now to give us a chance to go back to London and be happy?"

Again that unhappy glance between Carmichael and the housekeeper, but this time there was surprise with it.

"Shall I drive you back, Lisa? I don't suppose you'll want to stay here any longer today, will you? Some other time, when we've put that picture back in the attic where it belongs."

She shook her head slightly, still staring at it. "She was so beautiful," she murmured.

"That's the only thing people found to say about her," Carmichael said savagely.

"But they all loved her. You said so. Everyone says so. Except Nigel Franklin, and I don't think he could have known her very well. And Andrew can't bear to speak of her. And I've been deluding myself that I could take her place."

"You're wrong, Lisa," Carmichael said desperately. "It's not a question of taking her place. Can't you understand that?"

"Oh, isn't it," Lisa flashed. "Then can you explain how the old doctor works it out? He makes it plain that I'm an interloper."

"But that's different, Lisa. Oh, I really think I'll have to have a word with Andrew – if I get him to talk to me. He should be the one to clear all this up."

"How did she die? Can you bear to tell me that?"

"Does it matter?" he asked, and he looked harassed.

"It does, but if you can't bear to tell me, I daresay someone else will."

"She . . . had a fatal accident," he said painfully.

"I'm sorry, I'm so sorry, Carmichael. I didn't know," Lisa stammered. "I only thought that if I knew how, it might clear this up for always."

"Your best plan would be to go back to Andrew and forget all about it," Carmichael said, turning away.

"Would you like that cup of tea,

dear," Mrs. Reckless said, one eye on Carmichael.

"No. No, thanks, I'll be going home. As things are, I think I'd better find Andrew and have a talk with him."

Carmichael said he'd drive her back, but she didn't think he really wanted to, in case she started asking questions again. Besides, it was plain that he was busy outside, and had been dragged back by heaven-knew-what intuition to the housekeeper's room. Lisa remembered then that she had heard the telephone ring and his voice answer it, not far from the open door. After he had come off the telephone he must have heard what the housekeeper was saying about the picture. She said she'd catch a bus, and they told her if she hurried she might just do that. She was lucky, and saw it coming round the bend as she reached the crossroads.

It was just on lunch-time when she got back to The Old House. Andrew was washing his hands in the surgery. He called out, "Is that you, Lisa?"

She went straight through to him. "Oh, Andrew, do you think I could have a moment to talk to you? Alone, I mean."

"I think it would be a good idea," he said grimly. "I don't know where you've been and I haven't time to go into that now, but I must know about these pictures."

"What pictures?" she asked blankly.

He nodded towards the orange folder lying on his desk.

She picked it up, wonderingly and looked at the prints. "Why, they're all of me," she said blankly. Then her face lit up into a beautiful smile. "Oh, how kind of her, she must have got the film developed to send to me."

"She? Who are you talking about, Lisa?"

"Mrs. Smith. Roddy's mother. He *is* such a naughty boy and he's barely five. I caught him snapping me when he ought to have been taking pictures of the giraffe."

Andrew wanted desperately to believe her, but on the evidence, he didn't see how he could. Tobias had had that film and negatives; Tobias had known all about the trip to the Zoo and the other places. People in the town were hinting that Tobias had been in London with Lisa.

Even Mrs. Tabb hadn't been surprised at the story.

Mrs. Tabb stood outside the surgery door. "My good soup's cooling," she said, and it was at Lisa that she stared so disapprovingly.

"We can talk about this over lunch," Andrew said shortly.

But it was an unfortunate suggestion. Mrs. Tabb kept coming in and out, no doubt curious to know what was going on, and she kept looking affronted because they both broke off rather pointedly each time she entered the room.

In the end, Lisa burst out, "What you're trying to say is you think Tobias took these pictures. Is that it?"

"He said he did. They were in his possession. He gave them to me," Andrew said flatly. "This morning, in case you are wondering when, and he said I was to ask you about the time you spent with him on a water-bus and at the Tower of London, as well as the day at the Zoo."

Lisa was almost too angry to bother to explain. "Did he also tell you that he followed me, otherwise he wouldn't have known where to find me? Did he tell you he crashed in on my outing to the Zoo that I gave the little boy belonging to the Smiths – at Mrs. Cobb's suggestion, because they had been kind to her? Did he tell you that the first day I had on my own, wandering round the big stores, he followed me, snooping on me, until I got on that water-bus? I bet he didn't. Did he tell you I kept telling him to go away and leave me alone? I wish I'd approached the police now, and accused him of being a nuisance, though I suppose, being Tobias, he would have talked his way out of it and made me look a complete fool. Oh, what do you want, Mrs. Tabb? Can't you see we're having a private conversation?" she flared, in an altered tone, as she noticed that Mrs. Tabb had come quietly into the room and stood at the door behind Andrew, avidly listening.

"This concerns me just as much as it concerns you, miss," Mrs. Tabb said heatedly. "I've been in this family all my life; you're a newcomer, a stranger. You don't care about the Lees. I do. They *are* my life."

"Leave us, Mrs. Tabb," Andrew said wearily.

"No, let her stay, and perhaps she can explain her part in the reason why I was despatched to London so quickly. I heard you and your father talking – you were both working out how you could cash in on the fact that I was homesick for London and would be glad to go – and then you wouldn't have to admit that you were getting rid of me. I wasn't eavesdropping – I had just happened to come in at that point."

"She was listening," Mrs. Tabb said indignantly.

"And Mrs. Tabb persuaded Tobias to go into her kitchen with her and hide. And Mrs. Tabb told Tobias my address in London, so he could come after me. Otherwise how would he have known where I was?"

Mrs. Tabb met Andrew's enquiring glance as he got to his feet and faced her. "Of course I took Tobias into the kitchen. Didn't the dear doctor ask me to keep him under cover until we would arrange for him to sleep in Mr. Biddell's place?" she said calmly. "But as to telling him where Miss Lisa would be staying in London, why would I do that? The truth is, *she* told him. She was going with him. Ask her – she admitted to me that he picked her up in a bar."

"Lisa, that isn't true, is it?" Andrew asked her in a shocked voice.

Lisa was too angry to be coherent. "If this is not to be a private conversation, but you're going to allow the housekeeper to butt in, why don't you ask her for the reason why I was in that Bar, and bear in mind that I told her, of my own free will, honestly and truthfully."

"Well, Mrs. Tabb?" he asked, turning to her.

Mrs. Tabb shrugged. "Well, I would have thought, Master Andrew, that if a young woman frequents bars and admits to being picked up in one, then it doesn't much matter what flimsy excuse she afterwards gives for being there."

Lisa was shocked.

"All right, Andrew. So now you know. You either have to believe her, that I frequent bars and often get picked up, or you'll let me have the privilege of a private conversation with my own husband when I can give you my side without fear of interruption or having my story misrepresented."

"Oh, really, Lisa," he expostulated. "Do go out, Mrs. Tabb, and leave us alone. You had no business to come in on this. You've cleared away. What were you doing in here, anyway?"

"I've come to tell you someone wants you urgently," she said coldly. "They're at the back door now. Waiting."

He made a frustrated gesture to Lisa, and followed the housekeeper out of the room.

He was out all the afternoon. Afraid that the housekeeper would have something to say about the matter of the snapshots, Lisa quietly left the house and walked on the shore, thinking over what had happened at the farm and of all the things she had heard about Tressida Lee.

As Lisa saw it, there was no future for her in Queensmarket. She might just as well go back to No. 19. with a bit of dignity, but it did seem hard that Andrew had asked her to come back, on the excuse of wanting help, and then hadn't used it.

She stopped dead in her tracks as a new thought struck her. Had he really wanted her help? Or was it just to get her back here to find out what had been happening? How had he known about Tobias? Everything pointed to Mrs. Tabb. She must have been the first one to tell him that Tobias was in London.

Mrs. Tabb was no friend of hers, and Lisa was going to have this out with Andrew once and for all. And the only place she could have it out with him, without fear of interruption, was in their own bedroom.

She stayed out to tea. She had no stomach for tea at The Old House nor with any of her friends. She had it in a little tea-shop at the back of the town, where for once no-one seemed to know her or to take any notice of her. And her thoughts went over and over all the things she had heard about this family; fitting all the scraps together from the various sources. And there were still far too many gaps.

What if old Dr. Lee had married someone he didn't love, because his best friend had taken the girl he had wanted to marry? What if he had had two hopeless sons — Tobias the loafer, who couldn't leave other people's wives alone, and Quentin who didn't know which was his money and which anyone else's, and who had met his death in a plane over the North Sea while fleeing from justice? Surely, surely Dr. Lee shouldn't resent Lisa, who might not be attractive even, but who adored Andrew, and could, with a bit of freedom, try to make him happy?

Was the insidious charm of Tressida such that he couldn't bear to see anyone in her place? But Andrew hadn't felt like that, surely, or he wouldn't have married Lisa. No-one asked him to. She was his choice, as someone had rather pointedly said.

It was all a puzzle, and one that Lisa was determined to get to the bottom of.

She waited until she judged that evening surgery should be over, and then she went back. Rather than have another stand-up fight with Mrs. Tabb, she searched for and found another open window and got in. Mrs. Tabb could say it was a sneaky way of entering if she liked, but Lisa felt there wasn't much alternative.

If she had gone in the front way, Mrs. Tabb could have told her that Andrew was still with a patient. She might not have admitted who the patient was, but as least Lisa would have been saved from the ignominy of opening the surgery door to find Andrew in someone else's arms.

She couldn't have been more stunned if someone had hit her on the head with a rock. She just stood there staring. At any other time she would have noticed that the embrace was all on the girl's part, that Andrew looked as surprised and caught off guard as she herself felt, and that he was doing his best to thrust the girl away.

Indeed, before he turned to see Lisa at the open door, he said harshly to his patient, "What the devil are you playing at, Dinah?"

Dinah Gregory had seen Lisa by then. She recovered very quickly and said smartly, "Oh, look who's here!"

Before Andrew could do more than ejaculate: "Lisa!" Dinah continued, to Lisa, "I came over faint, and naturally I clung to Andrew. I knew him long before you did. There was no more in it than that — just a reflex action, I assure you — but in case you feel tempted to put your own construction on it, I would remind you to remember your own high jinks in London with Tobias — or doesn't Andrew know about that yet?"

Andrew said grimly, "Do come in, Lisa, don't just stand there. You get your things on, Dinah. I'll write you up something. My wife is supposed to be helping me in surgery, but next time you come I'll make sure of things by calling Mrs. Tabb in. It's your own fault."

"Don't be nasty, Andrew. You and I are such old friends, we don't have to go to such lengths, surely?"

"Don't we," he retorted.

After Dinah had gone, Andrew shut the door and stood with his back to it. "Well, you'd better say what you have to say, Lisa," he said, rather unfairly, she thought.

"I came to ask you if we could share the same room tonight, as being the only place sure of privacy, to thrash this whole matter out. It *was* necessary, Andrew, because of what happened today at Carmichael Mawson's place. But now it no longer seems to matter."

"What happened today?" he asked quickly.

She shook her head. "I can only repeat, it no longer matters. Whatever excuse you give for being in that situation with that girl, you can no more expect me to believe it than you believed me today when Mrs. Tabb said my reason for being in the Honey Bar was just an excuse. Besides, I seem to recall that when I told you Dinah Gregory had said in a loud voice to me in front those other people, that you had married me on the rebound and that you still loved your first wife, you told me that I was imagining it and that Dinah Gregory wouldn't say such a thing. You believed her and not me. And you furthermore humiliated me by going and telling her about it and asking her if it was the truth. You believed her and not me," she repeated.

"Well, I don't disbelieve you now about Dinah, but as to the Honey Bar – you must admit that your story wasn't very credible, Lisa. I thought perhaps you were scared and didn't want me to know you'd been to such a place, but you had been there, and you had let Tobias pick you up – ”

“I didn't. I walked out and left him. But on the strength of his having tried to pick me up in that Bar, he scraped an acquaintance later. You know him. You must know what a way he's got, and how he could make a woman look if she made a scene. Besides, he is your half-brother. I didn't want to be too nasty until I'd had a chance to speak to you about it.”

“That's just it, Lisa. That's what I can't forgive. You did have a chance and you didn't take it. You wouldn't have told me about it at all if I hadn't heard it from other people.”

“That means Mrs. Tabb, who sent him after me. Tobias himself,” Lisa said bitterly. “And you're wrong – I was sitting by the telephone in my house about to dial the number when you called me. I was going to ring you up and ask you if I could come back to Queensmarket because of Tobias. But you rang through yourself – didn't you think I was quick picking up the receiver?”

"But you didn't tell me about it," he accused her.

"Andrew, you were being nice to me. You sounded as if you really wanted me to come back. I was so overcome – it was so rare – I just grabbed at it with both hands. Why worry you about Tobias and spoil it all? How did I know he was going to follow me to the train and travel down with me? How did I know that he was going to act as if it was something quite different, so that that Mrs. Miggle would think we'd been great friends in London?"

"I wish I could believe you, Lisa," he said wretchedly. "The evidence is so strong against you, and you've had plenty of chances to tell me since – "

"What chances? If you're not being called out, Mrs. Tabb is dancing attendance on us. Why doesn't she want to leave us alone? What's she afraid of? It was she who tried to organise our sleeping arrangements, and it was she who said that – oh, what's the use? If I told you it would sound so outrageous that you'd never believe it. Either that woman has a bee in her bonnet about something, or she just shows she's plain possessive." She looked scornfully at him. "What an idiot I've been. I loved you so much, and all I wanted in the wide world was to share a little home with you, and to know where you were all day and to share your company at night. To bring up your children. It isn't much to ask, is it? And was it really so incredible that I should believe you really needed me when you asked me to come back? How wrong I was!"

"Who said you were wrong about it?" he retorted miserably, trying to think of a way to get through to her, to put all this right.

"You did, just now. I've just realised why you wanted me back. It was because you guessed that Dinah Gregory would be a nuisance, so you wanted me back to chaperone you. That's all. Goodness, what an ass I've been. Even Mrs. Cobb saw through her, though she hadn't met her. She knew when I told her — "

"You've talked to that woman about us?"

"No, just about the way Dinah Gregory treated me that day in the milk bar, and don't refer to Mrs. Cobb as *that woman.* She's one of the few friends I've got, and I'd have done better to stay with her."

Lisa stormed out of the room, almost knocking Mrs. Tabb over in her hurry. Afterwards she reflected that Mrs. Tabb must have been standing there, listening to all that, but at the time she thought of nothing but getting to her room to pack, to leave the house.

She lay on her bed, trying to stem the tears that would rush scalding down her cheeks. She mustn't look as if she'd been crying. She must be able to hold her head high when she walked out of this house, and not let the housekeeper see how crushed she was inside. Crushed with pain and the grief of knowing that she had lost Andrew – if she had ever had him.

She heard Andrew go out. She was used to coupling the sound of the telephone with his departing footsteps now, but on this occasion it had an ominous sound. Because of what she knew she must do, those were his footsteps going out of her life. She sat listening to them, and shaking all over.

She packed her overnight bag, but left the rest of her things for someone to send on later. She thought of writing a note, but she knew she'd never be able to think of the right things to say, in the time, if she were to catch the London train. She didn't want to stay in this house another night, and there was only one train left that would stop at Queensmarket.

Martin Bidell stopped her on her way to the station. "Where are you off to, Lisa, in such a rush?" he asked laughing. Then he saw her face, and caught at her arm.

"Don't stop me, Martin, or I'll lose my train," she said, and jerking free of him, she ran blindly across the road. It just happened to be clear at the time; Martin felt he wouldn't have rated her chances very high if a car had happened to be on the road. She just hadn't looked.

He decided to stop her on her mad flight, whatever was the cause. She couldn't go anywhere on her own like that. Her face was tear-stained, and she looked as if more tears weren't far off.

He got to the station just in time to see her pelting through the barrier. The train was about to start. She tugged open a door and someone helped her aboard before he could get a platform ticket.

He stood there thinking. Andrew, he knew, was out. He had spoken to him, as he had left. Come to think of it, Andrew had looked as if there might have been some trouble. Poor devil, what chance did he stand of putting things right in a row, with that telephone ringing all the time?

As he stood there, he saw Carmichael Mawson come out of the office with a parcel he had been to collect. "Mawson, just the chap to help," he said, buttonholing him and quickly telling him what had happened. "I can't think what on earth to do," he finished.

"I can – I'd better get to the junction and stop her if I can," Carmichael said. "I've got the big car here tonight. I just ought to be able to make it."

"You know what the trouble is, then?" Martin asked, bewildered.

"Got a fair idea – it's what happened at my place today," Carmichael yelled, as he got in his car and roared out of the yard.

Martin Biddell hesitated, and then went

back to The Old House and asked Mrs. Tabb to tell Dr. Lee he wanted to talk to him.

Dr. Lee was better this evening, and sitting up. Martin thought it was a pity he had to bring bad news. It would set the doctor back but it couldn't be helped.

"I've just seen Andrew go out," he said.

"Well, well, what of it, Martin? I had hoped you'd come to play Chess with me, not to keep me informed of my son's movements."

"He looked as if – well, he looked pretty much the same as when we got the news of Quentin's plane crash," Martin said quietly.

Dr. Lee's hand started to shake. "If that's all you can say, then you'd better go, Biddell."

"And I've just seen Lisa scramble on to the London train. She'd been crying," Martin went on.

Dr. Lee stared at. "All right, you know something. What's it all about?"

"I don't know, but Mawson does. He's driving to the junction to try to stop her. I daresay he'll do that, but whether he'll persuade her to come back here, is not for me to say."

"Mawson." Dr. Lee whispered the word and lay back. "Do you think she knows?"

"Not from me, she doesn't. Not from the Edwards' – Hazel assured me she had said very little indeed, in spite of Lisa's persistent questions. It's only natural that she'd want to know. I should have thought it would have been more fair to tell her."

"Why? What do *you* know about it?"

"I know Lisa. She's a nice girl. I think she would have made Andrew very happy, all things being equal."

"*Do* you. You don't know anything about it."

"I know that Tobias has done his best to wreck everything for them, and in case you've heard a garbled version from Mrs. Tabb, who is very pro-Tobias, I propose to tell you all I've heard about it."

Dr. Lee lay listening to Martin, and not breaking in on what he had to say.

"Are you sure of all this?" he asked at last.

"Quite sure. People like Lisa for herself.

Kidman's Mollie went so far as to appear from behind a curtain to ask to be taught music by Lisa."

"Bah, I don't believe it."

"I had it from Kidman himself. Kidman hadn't been very much impressed with all that make-up and the new hair style, but I understand you were at the back of that, Dr. Lee."

"I wasn't," he howled. "I only said to her – oh, well, what's it matter what I said? She came in looking pathetically eager to please, and so damned young that I felt a brute for just being there. So I lashed out at her, but I'm damned if I thought she'd go to a beauty place to get anything done about it."

"Well, she did, but she didn't like the one Hazel recommended. (I got all this from Hazel.) She got fed up and went to Skegwell and went slap into the very place where Tressida used to go. They started talking about her and that she went to the Honey Bar, so Lisa thought she'd like to see what sort of place the first wife went to. And she ran into a person who tried to pick her up. She cleared off, not liking it at all, but it seems that it was Tobias, and you know Tobias. He saw her later and took her up, and old Tabb didn't help, deliberately sending Tobias to London after her."

"Mrs. Tabb always did like Tobias," Dr. Lee allowed. "Well, it seems Fate is working against me, and that I shall have to make my peace with that girl. I shan't like it. I shall always see that beautiful creature haunting the place. I'll never get used to a new daughter-in-law."

"Well, I don't know, I daresay I've said more than enough already, Dr. Lee," Martin said, getting up, "but if it was me in your shoes, I think I'd try. For Andrew's sake."

He went then. An hour later, Carmichael Mawson drove Lisa to the door, and left her. "You won't want me around. I've done enough to you for one night," he said grimly.

Andrew was still out, and Mrs. Tabb was watching television. Martin hadn't disturbed her when he went. So far as she knew, Martin was still with the doctor. Martin thoughtfully left the door on the latch for Lisa, and looked out for her. He felt he could relax when he saw her get out of Carmichael's car.

She marched straight in to Dr. Lee's room. It was he that she wanted to talk to.

"I'd left Andrew. Carmichael brought me back. But if I can't get things clear, it will make no difference. I shall go tomorrow, and it will be for good."

"Oh, sit down, do. You're always standing over me in a threatening attitude," he begged her.

Lisa hardly noticed pulling up a chair and sitting by him. She was too busy marshalling her thoughts, planning what she must say to him.

"I saw her picture today for the first time — Tressida's. At Elmgates Farm. Mrs. Reckless had found it and put it up in her room. Carmichael was furious. There was a row. That was when I learned for the first time that his sister and Andrew's first wife were one and the same person."

Dr. Lee nodded.

"She was so beautiful. Everyone had warned me about that. I felt I never stood a chance of taking her place, from then onward."

He was silent, so she rushed on, "But Carmichael made me get off the train and he told me things about her and now I don't understand at all. He told me that she was the pilot of that little plane which Quentin came down in. She was helping him to escape."

Dr. Lee winced, but he said in a level tone, "Yes, she would, of course. She liked to cock a snoot at authority. She only meant to dump him on the Continent and come back and laugh at us all. That was her all over."

"And I'd heard before about her part in that awful business of knocking Mollie Kidman down and leaving her a cripple for life."

He nodded. "But she didn't do it deliberately," he felt bound to say, in the dead Tressida's defence.

"No. I know. That was what Carmichael said. She never meant any harm but she had that curse of leaving a trail of havoc behind her."

"Well, I don't know about that," the doctor said, thinking. "I have always said as loudly as the rest of them, that she never meant any harm, but now I wonder.

They picked her up out of the sea, but she died later. In hospital. And she was so surprised when she knew she couldn't last. She said it wasn't fair. Why not anyone else but not her. And she begged my son Andrew not to marry again."

He lay thinking about that. Lisa was too appalled to speak.

"I don't know what my son Andrew said to her but I know he didn't promise. She'd made him so unhappy. She'd refused him children. He wanted children."

"But he must have loved her once," Lisa whispered.

"I don't know. I know she chased him herself. She thought of the money, d'you see."

"Money? What money?"

"He hasn't told you? I suppose he wanted to make sure next time whether it was him or the money. He inherited a great deal from his mother. Oh, yes, Tressida wanted it, but she never got it out of him. He wasn't mean, but he didn't let her get her hands on the bulk of this fortune. That was set aside for his heart's dream. Do you know about that? Oh, well, perhaps it was early days to tell you.

Maybe he felt he was no longer sure of it coming true. I don't know. I only know that I wish I'd made it possible for him to open that clinic for his special cases. The children of the poor, the outcasts, the refugees, the misfits – him and his pathology." He sighed.

"So that was what he was talking about one evening," Lisa exclaimed, her eyes shining. "It was just before your letter came, asking him to come back here. Poor Andrew."

"Yes, poor Andrew. I stopped him, didn't I? And I suppose I pushed him into marrying Tressida. I loved having her around. You see, that girl I wanted to marry, all those years ago, was her mother. Just like her in looks. Like having Isabel around, just to see Tressida about. The same voice, the same pretty wilful ways. Mawson took her, took her from me. I had two wives later, but I never really got over Isabel. Perhaps I might have, if there had been no Tressida."

Lisa sat helplessly watching him, and everything she had ever heard about the Lees and the Mawsons clicked into place.

"Poppa, she called me, And she'd tease me, make me laugh, make me forget that she encouraged Tobias and aided Quentin in his nefarious practices. I couldn't be cross with her, for she'd ruffle my hair and play Chess with me – beat me at it, too. And she wanted that piano – I had it locked up when I heard you could play, but bless me, there wouldn't have been any touching point. She played modern stuff, and not very well, either, but her charm carried her through. You can have it, if you want it," he said suddenly.

"No. I wouldn't want it. And I'm not sleeping in her room any longer, that's if I stay, which I doubt. It depends on Andrew. But if I stay, it has to be on my terms. People must forget her. I'm not in her shoes. I'm on my own feet, and if people can't accept me, then I'm leaving." She got up. "Do you know where Andrew is? I can't trust Mrs. Tabb to tell me. She's as much my enemy as anyone."

"No," he sighed. "Not your enemy. Just enslaved by Tressida." And he told her where to find Andrew. "In the lighthouse. He went to lance Fred Olney's thumb. Why, what's the matter, girl? Are you ill? Come here – I can't reach you."

"I'm all right," she said, but she stopped with her eyes closed, holding onto the end of his bed. "It's the thought of going up those steps, I suppose. Nigel Franklin fell down them you know."

"The organist? Pah. Young fool. Fell, indeed. More likely young Hazel pushed him. Pair of hoydens. They'll get on all right, though. They understand each other." He peered anxiously at her. "Are you sure you're all right, child?"

It was the nearest he had ever got to an endearment, but there was no mistaking the tone of voice. He was no longer against her.

She smiled at him. That brilliant smile that had appealed so strongly to Martin, to Carmichael, Zillie Denner and the other friends she had made.

"Yes, I'm all right," she said.

"You didn't add 'Dr. Lee'. What's the matter? No more urge to fight me?" he said severely.

Andrew was being shown out, by Fred Olney, his hand heavily bandaged. Fred had yet to meet Lisa. He was enthusiastic.

"So this is Dr. Andrew's little lass, is it? You're a nice little thing. I'm right glad to meet you. Shake this other hand, will you? And you'd best come back with me and drink to the future because this is an occasion."

For some reason, Andrew agreed, and they went back to Fred's quarters, and then he insisted on them both going to the top to see the light. Lisa felt dreadful. The sea kept coming up, then dipping into a bottomless pit, and all she could do was to stand clinging to the rail, while the light went round and round, flicking its monotonous pattern. How long she could stand there, she didn't know.

At last, breaking in on Fred Olney's enthusiastic conversation, she said thickly, "Andrew, I'm not well. There's something I have to tell you. I've just come from your father — "

The way she said it made him think that his father had been taken ill again. "Then let's go — you'll excuse us, Fred?" Andrew said at once.

Lisa said, "But I can't manage — those — stairs — " and she pitched forward.

When she opened her eyes, she was down in Fred Olney's quarters. Fred wasn't there.

"He's with the light," Andrew said. "Lisa, tell me just how you feel."

"Oh, leave me alone," she said, trying to push him off. "Andrew, your father's talked to me, and Carmichael's talked – everyone's talked for the first time, and it's a pity they didn't before. I know everything, and if I hadn't run into Martin Biddell, I would be in London by now, and have left you."

He thought she was delirious. "Can you stand? If not, I'll have to carry you, but it's very clear that I must get you home."

His voice was gentle beneath its firm tone, and he had mentioned one significant word. "Home?" she repeated shakily. "You mean, you do believe me, about Tobias?"

"Oh, Lisa, did I ever say I disbelieved you? But I was hurt and angry that you didn't tell me about it before I heard it from other people," he said, gathering her up.

"Put me down," she said. "I think I

know what's wrong with me and all the rushing back to the surgery won't do much good. Listen, if Fred Olney isn't likely to interrupt us, for goodness' sake let's talk, privately, thrash it all out."

"All right," Andrew said, "let's."

Fred Olney wasn't used to being tactful. He lived alone mostly, and was used only to dealing with men. Men like himself, who had to handle shipwrecks, the sea, the weather – anything but a pretty woman and her distracted husband. He left them alone together for as long as he dared, then he felt he had to look to see what was going on. He found them locked in each other's arms, kissing. Kissing with such an intensity, oblivious to time and surroundings, that it shook Fred.

"Well," he said. "Well, I'll be jiggered," but he said it to himself as he toiled up all his steps again to the light. He wasn't wanted down there, that was clear. "Still," he told himself, "that's better than the last one. That Tressida Mawson-what-was. There was a tricky piece, if you like. All promise, and nothing made good. But this here one, well, that's different, eh? That's different."

Dr. Lee thought it was different, too, when Andrew came into his room later, an arm round Lisa. "Father, Lisa and I have talked it over," he began.

"So I can see," the doctor commented gruffly, looking at their happy faces. "I suppose you're clearing off to London, both of you?"

"No, Lisa thinks we ought to stay. We both want to. Here, with you. That's if you can put up with us, in view of what she's told me is going to happen, if all goes well."

"Um, and I suppose I'm not expected to know what that means. Well, the old man's a better doctor than you are, my fine fellow, for I knew what was wrong with her long ago."

"No, he didn't. He's cheating," Lisa said, laughing up into Andrew's face and twinkling across the bed at his father. "I nearly fainted in here, before I came to find you. And," she told Dr. Lee, "they made me walk to the top of the lighthouse, and I fainted properly that time."

Dr Lee, angrily shooting up his head roared at his son, "Made her do what? Have you no thought for my grandchild? Or are you such a poor doctor, you didn't see what was wrong with her?"

Lisa went to his side and dropped a shy kiss on his forehead, then left them both pleasantly wrangling about how she should be treated in the next half a dozen months.

Mrs. Tabb came out of the kitchen to her. "Dr. Lee's been talking to me, Miss Lisa," she began. She was climbing down, and it was a very painful business for her, but generously, Lisa helped her.

"Don't mention it, Mrs. Tabb. Let's let bygones be bygones. I'd like that. And besides, I'm going to have a baby."

A baby. It was a song in Lisa's heart.

They ensonced her in the great bed in the big room, freshly decorated, and they fussed over her, in spite of her protests. And while she waited for Andrew to come up and take his place by her side, she lay listening to the sea and the wind, and watched through the chink in the curtains the light flicking across the North Sea, and she said softly, "You've lost, Tressida.

You can't haunt me any more. You only took, but I've got so much to *give*, and I've got Andrew's heart."

THE END

Other titles in the Ulverscroft Large Print Series:

TO FIGHT THE WILD
Rod Ansell and Rachel Percy

Lost in uncharted Australian bush, Rod Ansell survived by hunting and trapping wild animals, improvising shelter and using all the bushman's skills he knew.

COROMANDEL
Pat Barr

India in the 1830s is a hot, uncomfortable place, where the East India Company still rules. Amelia and her new husband find themselves caught up in the animosities which seethe between the old order and the new.

THE SMALL PARTY
Lillian Beckwith

A frightening journey to safety begins for Ruth and her small party as their island is caught up in the dangers of armed insurrection.

CLOUD OVER MALVERTON
Nancy Buckingham

Dulcie soon realises that something is seriously wrong at Malverton, and when violence strikes she is horrified to find herself under suspicion of murder.

AFTER THOUGHTS
Max Bygraves

The Cockney entertainer tells stories of his East End childhood, of his RAF days, and his post-war showbusiness successes and friendships with fellow comedians.

MOONLIGHT AND MARCH ROSES
D. Y. Cameron

Lynn's search to trace a missing girl takes her to Spain, where she meets Clive Hendon. While untangling the situation, she untangles her emotions and decides on her own future.

THE TWILIGHT MAN
Frank Gruber

Jim Rand lives alone in the California desert awaiting death. Into his hermit existence comes a teenage girl who blows both his past and his brief future wide open.

DOG IN THE DARK
Gerald Hammond

Jim Cunningham breeds and trains gun dogs, and his antagonism towards the devotees of show spaniels earns him many enemies. So when one of them is found murdered, the police are on his doorstep within hours.

THE RED KNIGHT
Geoffrey Moxon

When he finds himself a pawn on the chessboard of international espionage with his family in constant danger, Guy Trent becomes embroiled in moves and countermoves which may mean life or death for Western scientists.

MORNING IS BREAKING
Lesley Denny

The growing frenzy of war catapults Diane Clements into a clandestine marriage and separation with a German refugee.

LAST BUS TO WOODSTOCK
Colin Dexter

A girl's body is discovered huddled in the courtyard of a Woodstock pub, and Detective Chief Inspector Morse and Sergeant Lewis are hunting a rapist and a murderer.

THE STUBBORN TIDE
Anne Durham

Everyone advised Carol not to grieve so excessively over her cousin's death. She might have followed their advice if the man she loved thought that way about her, but another girl came first in his affections.

DEATH TRAIN

Robert Byrne

The tale of a freight train out of control and leaking a paralytic nerve gas that turns America's West into a scene of chemical catastrophe in which whole towns are rendered helpless.

THE ADVENTURE OF THE CHRISTMAS PUDDING

Agatha Christie

In the introduction to this short story collection the author wrote "This book of Christmas fare may be described as 'The Chef's Selection'. I am the Chef!"

RETURN TO BALANDRA

Grace Driver

Returning to her Caribbean island home, Suzanne looks forward to being with her parents again, but most of all she longs to see Wim van Branden, a coffee planter she has known all her life.

IN PALE BATTALIONS
Robert Goddard

Leonora Galloway has waited all her life to learn the truth about her father, slain on the Somme before she was born, the truth about the death of her mother and the mystery of an unsolved wartime murder.

A DREAM FOR TOMORROW
Grace Goodwin

In her new position as resident nurse at Coombe Magna, Karen Stevens has to bear the emnity of the beautiful Lisa, secretary to the doctor-on-call.

AFTER EMMA
Sheila Hocken

Following the author's previous autobiographies – EMMA & I, and EMMA & Co., she relates more of the hilarious (and sometimes despairing) antics of her guide dogs.